ANNE FINE

The Book of the
Banshee

CORGI BOOKS

THE BOOK OF THE BANSHEE
A CORGI BOOK 0 552 55303 4
978 0 552 55303 2 (from January 2007)

First published in Great Britain 1991 by Hamish Hamilton Ltd
Corgi edition published 2006

3 5 7 9 10 8 6 4 2

Papers used by Random House Children's Books are natural, recyclable
products made from wood grown in sustainable forests.
The manufacturing processes conform to the environmental regulations
of the country of origin.

Set in 12/16pt Gioconda by
Falcon Oast Graphic Art Ltd.

Corgi Books are published by Random House Children's Books,
61–63 Uxbridge Road, London W5 5SA,
a division of The Random House Group Ltd,
in Australia by Random House Australia (Pty) Ltd,
20 Alfred Street, Milsons Point, Sydney, NSW 2061, Australia,
in New Zealand by Random House New Zealand Ltd,
18 Poland Road, Glenfield, Auckland 10, New Zealand,
and in South Africa by Random House (Pty) Ltd,
Isle of Houghton, corner of Boundary Road & Carse O'Gowrie,
Houghton 2198, South Africa

THE RANDOM HOUSE GROUP Limited Reg. No. 954009
www.kidsatrandomhouse.co.uk

A CIP catalogue record for this book is available from the British Library.

Printed and bound in Great Britain by
Cox & Wyman Ltd, Reading, Berkshire

*For Brigadier Richard Warren,
with love and gratitude*

I am indebted to Thomas Suthren Hope for his magnificent account of his time in the trenches, *The Winding Road Unfolds,* Putnam, London, 1937.

Chapter 1

Today a writer came to school and gave a talk to our class and 3B. No one was expecting her, that was quite obvious. Chopper and I noticed her standing about in the entrance hall, waiting for Mrs MacKay to think of someone who might be able to take her off her hands. Chopper thought she was a new teacher, so he took an interest. I pointed out that she couldn't have come for an interview, the bag on the floor beside her was far too full. And she couldn't have come to start teaching, either. No one turns up at lunchtime on their first day.

Then we heard Mrs MacKay rap smartly on her glass screen as Scotbags strolled through the swing doors.

'Mr Scotbeg. Mr Scotbeg! Here's—'

She stopped. She wasn't sure what to call her.

The woman put on a bit of a patient look.

'Alicia Whitley,' she said. 'I'm Alicia Whitley.'

She didn't say if she was Miss or Ms or Mrs, and so she didn't really help poor Mrs MacKay at all. I got the feeling that was deliberate. Alicia Whitley just stood there, watching, with her skirts swaying and her hands stuck deep in her jacket pockets, and all of a sudden I wanted to stay near enough to find out what happened. So nudging Chopper in case he sailed off to registration without me, I dropped on one knee and fiddled with a shoelace. Chopper caught on, and started to inspect the photo of last year's girls' hockey eleven. Give Chopper his due, he's not very bright, but he always knows when I want to hang about and eavesdrop.

'Mrs Whitley,' said Mrs MacKay. (If she can't work out if someone's married or not, she always pretends they are. She thinks it's much nicer.)

Scotbags looked blank. He kept his blank look on just long enough to let Alicia Whitley know he hadn't the faintest idea who she was, and needed enlightening. Then he switched channels to his 'affable headmaster' act, all smiles and outstretched paw.

'Good morning, Mrs Whitley. Or should I

say . . . (nod at the clock, pause, throaty chuckle) . . . afternoon?'

It was exactly one fifty. Afternoon bell.

You could see Ms Whitley decide to crack, before Scotbags' lengthy brainsearch for some clue as to why she was standing there was extended through some tortuous chat about the weather.

'I'm Alicia Whitley the writer,' she told him. She said the word 'writer' quite clearly, so he couldn't miss or ignore it. 'I've come as arranged four months ago. By Miss Adulewebe.'

'Miss Adulewebe?'

'That's right.' In case he started arguing, she pulled an envelope with the school crest out of her jacket pocket, slid out a letter, unfolded it and took a look. 'Miss *Lorna* Adulewebe.'

Was she teasing Old Scotbags? No school would have two Miss Adulewebes, after all.

'Miss Adulewebe,' groaned Scotbags. He tried not to groan it too badly, but it showed. Miss Adulewebe taught here at Wallace School for only two terms, but she certainly did leave her mark on poor Scotbags. He can't stand teachers who go around arranging things. It makes work for him, and the man hates work. He thinks he's paid to walk about smiling and sticking out his paw.

But Alicia Whitley was getting fed up now.

'Here I am, then,' she announced. 'As arranged. In writing. Several months ago. So I suggest you simply show me to your school library, clear me a table, bring in no more than sixty pupils to whom I'll speak about the business of writing books, and then you can come back and fetch them an hour and a half later.'

It must have sounded simple enough, even to Scotbags. But he hates arrangements so much he'd obviously have preferred to send her packing with a regretful shrug, and one last affable smile. Perhaps she sensed that, because she suddenly reached down for her enormous bag.

'After all,' she added lightly. 'You'll have to *pay* me. There's no question about that. So some of your pupils may as well benefit from my going to the trouble of driving all this distance.'

Beside me, Chopper whistled gently through clenched teeth. He's not bright, but he's not stupid. He recognizes a good Scotbagging when he hears it.

And Mr Scotbeg, too, knows when he's beaten. 'Flowers!' he yelled.

'Yes, sir!' By now I'd absentmindedly tied one of my shoelaces into a massive and unsightly knot.

'Pick up this lady's bag and show her to the library. Put out sixty chairs, and clear a table.'

'Yes, sir.'

'Chopper!'

He's odd that way, Scotbags. He yells at me by my surname for all the world as if he were the whiskery headmaster in some strict old boarding school, and then bellows 'Chopper!', which is only a nickname.

'Yes, sir?'

'You're a 3P, aren't you? Nip along and tell Miss Shaw to send your lot to the library as soon as second bell rings. Then go and ask Mr Astley if he wants to send 3B as well.'

Get that? Alicia Whitley isn't expecting anyone in particular. She probably couldn't care. It makes sense to send 3B. Mr Astley loves knocking off. Any excuse. They once stopped for twenty minutes to look at a rainbow. But 'tell Miss Shaw to send your lot'! Does Scotbags bother to stroll along and check that Miss Shaw hasn't spent her entire lunch break setting out complicated apparatus for an experiment, or arranging her slides in order and fixing up the screen and the projector? No, he doesn't. He picks on Miss Shaw because she's the most timid member of staff, and wrecks any plans she might have made without so much as an apology.

Why should I mind? I hate chemistry. So I just bent down and picked up the bag. It weighed so much I thought she must keep bricks in it.

'This way,' I said.

'Are you a threepy or a threeby?' she asked. (That's how she pronounced them. I got the feeling that was how she thought of us: threepies and threebies.)

I tried to say 'I'm a 3P.' But it came out a bit threepy, and that is how I've thought of it ever since.

'And how old are you?'

This wasn't interest in me. I understood that. It was a quick check over the battleground. Clearly this lady had been in secondary schools before. When I told her, she filed the information away, nodding.

'And what was the last book you read?'

I wasn't going to tell her that. The last book I read was the one I read every night now. I bought it seven months ago in a book sale at our branch library. Mum wouldn't go. She says it's too depressing to watch our national heritage being sold off like jumble by the new District Barbarian, but she did give me fifty pence to see if I could pick up a nice Stephen King horror to take her mind off Estelle. (Estelle is my sister.) On the big trestle tables I found a book by William Scott Saffery, *The Longest Summer*. I just picked it up and opened it.

In front of me there's nothing but darkness, then flashes of the guns to right and left. Above my head, one howling banshee shell after another spins past, and the crump of their bursting makes the ground shudder. I know I face the unknown – danger, hardship, wounds, maybe even my own death. But the thought of this fails to touch me. I can think only of heroics, of battles won, of this great war I've read so much about, and for so long, in every newspaper that came to hand. What if I had missed it? What if I had been born too late? No need to worry now, for I am here – proud and glad – and that is all that matters. This will be my greatest adventure.

I didn't read any further. I simply tucked *The Longest Summer* firmly under my arm. And though I spent at least an hour longer at the sale, picking up all sorts of books and carrying them about a bit before exchanging them for others (no Stephen Kings, of course. As Mum said sarcastically when I got home, the District Barbarian would never sell *them* off), that was the only book I never put down again, not even once.

It's been under my bed ever since. I hardly read anything else now. I read a chunk of it each night before I put out the light and go to sleep. I can't work out what it is exactly, but the book haunts me. William Saffery was no older than I am when he lied to the army about his age. He claimed he was eighteen. (This was the middle of the First World War, when men were dying in their thousands, so the army wasn't checking.) He starts off merrily enough. He's sitting on the back of a lorry watching the long and winding road unfold behind him – like a grey ribbon, he says – and he's excited and keen. Of course, within a couple of days I was a lot further into the book, and he was a lot further into the war . . .

But I don't want to talk about any of that to someone I've never even met before, who only wants to know what I'm reading so she can work out what sort of school she's in, and what she's going to talk about for a whole double period.

So I skipped back a month or so.

'One of the last books I read was *Right Ho, Jeeves*,' I told her. 'Before that, I read *Bagthorpes Haunted*, and before that, *The Viz Annual*. I always have to read to my little sister, Muffy, when I put her to bed. She's into *Rumpelstiltskin*. I read half of *Flowers in the Attic*, but I only got that far through because my name's Will Flowers, so it was a bit of a joke to carry it around for a day or two. We're reading *Far From the Madding Crowd* in class, but I went and finished that at home one night, so while they're all ploughing through it I read *Escape from Colditz* under the desk.'

She looked delighted. I don't think I've ever pleased anyone so easily in my whole life.

'But that's just me,' I said. 'Chopper hasn't read a book the whole time I've known him, and some of the others *can't* even read, let alone *won't*.'

We'd reached the library by now. I swung her bag of rocks up on a table.

'You'd better not judge by me,' I warned.

'Thanks,' she said.

She meant thanks for warning her, I could tell. She didn't mean thanks for carrying the rock bag. She could have done that perfectly well by herself. She was only being polite back there, letting Old Scotbags pretend that she couldn't.

She looked around. It's not a bad library. It's got a few bookshelves with a few books on them. You can't say fairer than that.

I started on the chairs. She touched my arm.

'Listen,' she said. 'I'll do the chairs. You be a poppet and find me a cup of coffee.'

Be a poppet! I couldn't believe it. My mother calls Muffy 'poppet'. Muffy is four!

I went, though. I didn't really have much choice. But I made the mistake of calling in at my classroom first for registration, and got caught up in one of The Animal Astley's endless time-wasting inquisitions.

'You're going to fetch *coffee*?'

'It's not for me. It's for Alicia Whitley, the writer.'

'Is that this woman Chopper claims is sitting in the library, waiting for you lot and 3B? What is she planning to do with you?'

'I don't know. Talk to us, I suppose. About her books.'

'But you haven't been reading any books by Alexa Whitchurch. You lot have been reading *Far From the Maddening Crowd*.'

'*Madding*,' I corrected him. '*Far From the Madding Crowd*.'

'*Maddening*,' he insisted. 'I work in this bear garden. I ought to know.' He turned to the rest of the class and started bothering them instead of me.

'Hands up anyone who's ever read a book by someone called Alice Whitford.'

Marisa began to put up her hand in a soppy kind of way; but as soon as she realized we were all looking at her, she pulled it down again, sharpish.

Mr Astley grunted.

'Good luck to Alison Whitfield,' he said. 'The poor woman probably doesn't know what she's in for. I suppose I'd better come along and watch her back for her.'

He sighed.

'Go along, then! Fetch her coffee!'

On the way back to the library I ran into the stragglers from 3B and, what with their stupid fooling, spilled nearly all the coffee. But I got what was left to Alicia Whitley just as the rest of them were trailing in. She took it gratefully.

'Thanks, Will.'

I was relieved she didn't call me 'poppet' again,

in front of all the others. But I was also pleased that she'd remembered my name. (It took Mr Astley a whole term.) Chopper had saved a seat for me at the back. When I sat down on it, he was already slumped well down in his own place, staring gloomily at his huge feet.

'A whole double period,' he groaned. 'About books!'

It must be hard if you can barely read.

She'd put her coffee cup down. Mr Astley stood up to sort us out, but she took one look at him and brushed him aside. It's not as if he could do much of a job of introducing her to us anyhow. He didn't know who she was. So she just stood up and dispensed with his services with a polite little wave. He wasn't a bit put out. He's not a sulker, and he knows when he's well off. Gratefully, he subsided onto his chair, and surreptitiously opened one of the files that he'd brought along with him so, if he got bored, he could get on with whatever it was he was doing.

Swirling her skirts, she started up.

'My name's Alicia Whitley.'

That, in itself, caught most people's attention. We spend whole periods pestering the staff to tell us their first names. When you hear someone her age just stand up and announce theirs, you take a bit of interest.

'I'm a writer,' she went on. 'That's how I earn my living and I'm going to talk to you about writing books.'

Chopper let out a groan. It was only a little one, a tiny one really. But she still heard it at the front.

She stopped dead.

'Chopper!' she ordered. 'Come down and sit here.'

She pointed to the row of empty seats at the front.

Chopper was astonished. So was everyone else (including Mr Astley). I knew already just how quick she was with names, and she'd heard Chopper's, of course, when Scotbags bellowed at him. But as I've already mentioned, Chopper's not bright, and in the shock of the moment he forgot that.

He stood up, beet-red and nervous.

'Chum me!' he whispered, desperate.

So I stood up, too, and together we threaded our way to the front between the chairs she'd just shoved out in careless wavy rows. Mr Astley stirred in his seat. I thought for a moment he was about to speak up and send me back. You know the sort of thing. 'Excuse me! I don't believe I heard anybody mentioning *your* name . . .' But it was as if Alicia Whitley saw it coming, and once again she seemed quite amiably to wave him aside.

'I'll let Will come with you, Chopper, just so long as you both listen.'

There was an unmistakable notch-up of tension. You could tell what they were all thinking: 'Does this woman know *everyone*'s name?' And then they all settled down. You can sense it. It is a sort of 'not worth bothering to make trouble' mood. I don't know how it works. Maybe the bright ones relax because they know that someone's in control and, just for once, everything isn't going to get spoiled and we might even get some real work done. The piggies in the middle are always happy to be entertained. They're easy settlers. The thicks go off into daydreams, and, most miraculous of all, the trouble-makers set about fiddling fairly quietly with something that can safely be ignored.

Chopper sprawled on his new chair, sunk in the deepest despair. And I – I stared at Alicia Whitley.

I was all ears.

* * *

I don't know what it was that interested me so much. Part of it might have been that she talked so fast. She talked a blue streak, at about a hundred miles an hour, and that made it feel as if it wasn't just another boring lesson. Most of the teachers I've had talk horribly slowly. Some of them actually come out with the words at half speed, and others sound as if they're talking normally at first, but when you pay attention you realize that they're repeating themselves over and over again, first for the thicks in the back row, and then for all the people who've only just come in because they've been mucking about in the changing rooms, and then, one last time, for all those who've been there the whole time but simply weren't bothering to listen.

She talked fast, but she never said the same thing twice, so if you weren't paying attention – bad luck, *poof!* you missed it. She talked so fast you practically had to sit up straight to hear. She pulled one thing after another out of the bag to show us. Mucky scribbled sheets of paper with huge crossings-out that she said were the first go at the first pages, written at top speed, just to get into it.

She showed us pages written a bit more neatly, later, with grubby patches where she'd rubbed out over and over again to try things around different ways. On some of the sheets she'd rubbed things out so often she had giant holes in the paper.

'April,' she said.

She kept talking, all about how she kept at it, day after day, week after week, month after month. Then she showed us pages she'd typed up and printed out, all smart and clean.

'September,' she said.

I thought we must be pretty well through by now. But, no. Almost at once she held up a matching sheet, but this one was covered with pencilled corrections and crossings-out and additions. She'd clearly been at it all over again.

'October,' she told us. 'But we are getting there.'

November was pretty neat. It was all printed out beautifully, and it was only because I was in the front row that I could see splodges on the paper where the light hit the back and showed she'd been using correction fluid to blot out a comma or two, rather than go to the trouble of printing the whole page out again.

Then, suddenly, she swooped in the bag again and pulled out a large green file. On the front was a label that said in big letters: *The Rise and Hard Fall of Stewart Moffat.*

'December!' she said triumphantly.

'Alec Whitsun!' I said, astonished.

It just came out. I couldn't help it.

She stared at me. First she looked pleased, then anxious. She broke off talking to everybody for a second, and dipping in front of me, her skirts brushing the floor, she asked:

'You don't mind?'

'Oh, no,' I said. I was really embarrassed now. 'Not at all.' And just as she rose to her full height, I added stupidly: 'Sorry.'

I knew exactly what she meant, though, when she asked 'Do you mind?' She was worried in case it would spoil the books for me, knowing they'd been written by an Alicia, not an Alec. I've read all ten Whitsun books. I think they're brilliant. For years I thought that there were only four. Then one day, purely by accident, I found another, and in the front of that there was a list – 'Other Books by Alec Whitsun' – with six more titles I had never seen, including *The Rise and Hard Fall of Stewart Moffat.* It took me ages to get hold of all of them because the Alec Whitsuns were the sort of books people grab straight off the library trolley and don't put down in case someone else makes off with them. It was so odd to think he was standing there – *she* was standing there – holding a file of pages that she'd written over and over, and then typed, and I'd read through school and supper and late into the night, with all my pillows pushed up against the bottom of the door, to stop Mum and Dad from noticing I hadn't put my light out.

'Questions?' she said suddenly.

It didn't seem to occur to her there might not be any. She obviously thought writing books was the most interesting topic in the whole world. She didn't even seem bothered by the long, embarrassed silence that followed. I expect she thought we were all busy working out the best way of asking our questions.

Marisa put up her hand first, of course.

'Can *anyone* be a writer?' (She meant her.)

Ms Whitley got her teeth into that one, I can tell you. There were writers and writers, she said, but you couldn't be a *good* one unless you were a good reader. That was essential. 'You're writing for the reader in yourself,' she said. 'You've got to know when it works. If you don't read, if you can't recognize when something's *right*, how can you do it yourself?'

It was true, what she was saying. I knew that. I'd known it from the moment I opened up *The Longest Summer* and read a bit of it. You know at once when something's written right. Something inside you says: 'Yes! That's *exactly* how it must have been. That's how it would have *felt*.' And she knew too. She stood there talking about it with the same mad light in her eyes as that funny Welshman who preaches in the arcade on Saturdays. And she told us the one other thing that we needed.

'You've got to have something to tell, too. It could be a good story. Or something funny. Maybe it's something that's been on your mind, something you're working out. You want to write about it anyway. It doesn't matter what it is, but it does help a bit if it's something that matters.'

You work that out. I had a go at it as the last bell rang, and Mr Astley hastily snapped shut his file, leaped to his feet, and thanked Alexandra Whitburn for her most interesting and inform- ative talk. She was right again, I decided. You have to have something to write about. William Scott Saffery had his five months in the trenches. What he has to tell is so amazing I read about it over and over again. I can't stop. I know his days and nights now a whole lot better than I know my own. Somehow I couldn't imagine him squatting in all that mud and blood and rain, reading about *my* life.

But then again, why not? I would. If I were in his place, I would have given the world to read myself out of it whenever I could. The week Stormer Phillips threatened to get his brother's gang to rough me up, I think I read all the time. If I were William Saffery, I'd snatch up anything that might take my mind off the infernal pounding of the guns.

And our house is a battleground too, in its own way. That's what Mum says, at least. She claims that since Estelle turned into a shrieking banshee overnight, our house has been hell on earth. Sometimes Mum gets so rattled about Estelle, she won't even come in the door like a normal human being. She parks the car a little way along the street, creeps up to the house, and taps on the window where I sit to do my homework.

I open it and lean out. Mum's usually standing in the flower bed, with mud all over her shoes. She doesn't ask me how my day at school went. Oh, no. No time for niceties under fire. She just gets straight to the point.

'How's your sister?'

I know she doesn't mean Muffy, that's for sure.

'She's in a bit of a mood.'

A hunted look comes over Mum's face.

'Where is she? Upstairs?'

'No. She's in the kitchen, waiting for you to come home.'

'Oh, God. Help me in.'

I can't imagine what the neighbours think, seeing her hitching up her skirt and clambering in through the window, day after day. Mum says if they've ever had a teenage daughter they'll understand at once, and if they haven't there's no point in even trying to explain.

'All I need is five minutes,' she says. 'Five minutes' peace and quiet. Then I can face it.'

'They gave them rum in the trenches.'

'Trenches!'

The way she says it, you'd think she'd happily sell the whole house (with Estelle in it) to get a nice quiet trench on the front line.

Battles at home and abroad. All good to read about. The more I thought about it, the surer I was that William Scott Saffery would be just as riveted by my tale as I am by his. I thought at first it was just a fleeting idea, something that drifts across your mind and away, like one of those transparent wavy worm things that float down in front of your eyes in harsh sunlight. It was only when all the rest of them started scuffling around under their chairs for their bags, and barging one another on the way to the swing doors to get back to the classrooms to pack up, that I realized what I had done. I had made a decision.

When William Saffery found himself in the middle of a war, he sat down and wrote a book about it.

And so would I.

Chapter 2

William Saffery wrote on 'anything that would take writing'. I've got a beautiful black book. The cover is canvas with a glossy sheen. On the front, in gold block letters, it says THE BESHOOHOEFTE BANK, and I found it in a rubbish skip outside Mum's offices a few years ago. Only the first seven pages had anything on them at all, and that was some strange old foreign accounts in spidery brown writing. I tore them out with the back halves that would have fallen out later, then I kept the book at the bottom of my cupboard. Each time Estelle went rooting through my stuff, looking for something to wear, she'd ask me if she could have it. I always said no. I knew it would come in useful. Ideally, of course, the book I write should be called *The Beshoohoefte Bank*, but I have a different title in mind. I won't let on yet, though. As William Scott Saffery says on his first page:

> *On account of military regulations,*
> *occasional gaps in this story are*
> *unavoidable.*

I can't miss everything out though, however dangerous it would be if it were found. And dangerous is the word. Estelle's a year younger than I am, and half a head shorter, but she still scares me stiff when she loses her temper.

And she would kill me if she found this and read it. So it's a good thing I've been reading all these 'Escape from Colditz' books, and learned how to hide things from serious snoopers. Mum and Dad stroll in here often enough, of course, spooning out laundry and fretting about that patch of furry green mould struggling its way up the side wall. But since Mum went back to work after Muffy, I've had to do my own cleaning. One fluff ball too many and my pocket money is slashed to almost nothing; but at least no one else goes hoover-nozzling round my furniture.

I'll keep the book under the carpet beneath my bed, hidden well away in the corner. Estelle won't find it there. At least, I hope she won't. She'd hit the roof, just reading what I've written so far. The trouble is, she's got no sense of humour any more. She used to be good fun. But since the day I gave her that badge that said 'Terrible Teens' and she took it straight off the card backing and stabbed me with the pin, Estelle has changed. Sometimes she's almost as sweet and easy-going as she used to be. But most of the time it's like sharing a home with some apprentice witch. We live in constant fear. Everyone in the family has their own way of describing what happens to Estelle. 'Goes a bit awkward' is Dad's phrase. Mum is more direct. She claims Estelle curdles. Gran offers warily: 'Gets a bit – *difficult* – at times . . .' Muffy says nothing, of course. (Muffy hardly ever speaks.) But the way she sometimes sticks her thumb in her mouth and stares at Estelle as if she were something really weird on the telly makes it perfectly clear that, like everyone else in the family, she's wondering what's happening to her favourite person.

Because Estelle was always an angel before, everyone's agreed on that. She was such a perfect angel that, even though I'm a whole year older, she was the one they always put in charge. 'Be sure and hold Will's hand crossing the main road, Estelle' turned out to mean her looking after me, and not, as I assumed for years, me looking after her. In fact, Mum claims Estelle practically brought me up. She's been brilliant at looking after others since she was tiny. Part of it comes from the fact that I was a bit of a late bloomer, of course. But a lot of it comes from her soft heart.

And she was born with that. Why, when she was only eighteen months old, Dad put his back out on holiday, dumping her in a hotel cot. He lay spreadeagled, quite unable to move. Estelle couldn't reach him to pat him better through the bars, so she pulled herself up and leaned over the top rail. Dad says the last thing he recalls before he passed out was Estelle's hot little tears of sympathy splashing on his bare back. Whenever anyone even mentions Tossa Del Mar now, Dad's eyes fill up. He always claims that it's the memory of the excruciating pain, but we know better. Dad's soppy about Estelle, and always has been.

Mum's full of stories about how wonderful she was back in the old days, as well.

'Such a clever little thing! Do you know, once, when she was sneaking biscuits out of a packet I'd left on the table, I turned round from the sink and asked her: "Estelle, is that your fourth or your fifth?" Guess what she answered. "Oh, dear! I think it's probably my last!"' Gran rabbits on about the frilly pink frocks that made Estelle look so enchanting. Now she goes around half the time looking like something that just crawled out of a grave, if you want Gran's opinion. And even Chopper (who's been out with practically every girl in the school, so ought to be able to judge) admits that Estelle *used* to be all right.

So what do *I* think?

I can't understand what's happened. I always thought that people grew up bit by bit, staying much the same inside, but learning things one at a time in a steady progression. So whatever it is that's happening to Estelle worries me. How *can* someone already know that you have to ask other people before you take their stuff and muck about with it, and then seem suddenly to forget overnight how that person will feel if they walk into a room and find their precious radio, or calculator, or new leather jacket, carelessly strewn on the floor? How can someone go to the same school, term after term, and then just forget all the rules? And how come Estelle can walk into a room and see me – a brother she's lived with amiably enough for years – and suddenly start snarling? What's wrong with me all of a sudden? I'm just the same. I'm getting taller every week, but there's no reason that should bother Estelle. After all, it's me who keeps banging my head on things, not her. Yesterday I walked into the kitchen and Mum said:

'Will, your hair's gone bright yellow!'

It was turmeric. I bash my head on things so often now, I scarcely notice the pain. I'd knocked the underside of the spice shelf as I went past, and all the turmeric had puffed out of its little plastic tub, and landed all over my hair.

So I have my own problems. She's not the only one round here who's doing some changing. I'm growing a lot faster than she is. But I don't think that I am changing inside. I think I'm still the person I always was. I certainly haven't turned into a banshee, like she has.

You take this morning. That was typical. Monday is Mum's day off. Muffy stays home. So, now that Dad keeps the garage open all weekend, Monday's the only morning he and Mum ever get to lie in. She's sitting up in bed, drinking the tea I'd brought her, and Dad was still rolled in the downie, dead to the world.

Then Estelle starts. I saw the whole thing because I was rooting through Mum's purse, looking for lunch money she swore must be in there somewhere. Estelle sailed in. She didn't say 'Good morning' or anything. She just started in on them.

'I need six pounds.'

I looked up. I was in time to see Mum's face set, and her fingers stiffen round the handle of her teacup.

'Oh, yes?'

'Yes.'

No explanation, you notice. Just 'I need six pounds'. Under the downie I saw the little bulge of Mum's foot slide across to touch Dad's leg. I knew exactly what that meant. It meant: 'You're her father, George Flowers. Wake up and deal with this. It's too early for me. I can't face it.'

Dad knew what it meant, too. Sighing, he rolled over, bringing the downie with him, like a beached whale. He opened one bleary eye. By then, Estelle had plonked herself down at the dressing table, and started fiddling with Mum's precious make-up.

Dad made an effort.

'Six pounds?'

'By this morning!'

Somehow Estelle managed to make it sound like some impatient kidnapper's last reasonable offer before he started sending severed ears through the post to the distressed family.

'But what's it for?'

All of a sudden Estelle was scowling in the mirror as if Dad had just accused her of being a liar and a thief, not simply asked her why she needed six pounds.

'For a field trip! I *told* you!'

'Not sure you did, Estelle . . .'

He wouldn't be that tactful with me, I can tell you. If I came up to him demanding money with menaces, he wouldn't bite his tongue and say, 'Not sure you did, Will.' He'd say straight out: 'No, you didn't. I'm not deaf. And I'm not stupid, either!' But like everyone else in the family over the last few months, Dad has become quite wary of Estelle. Like William Saffery, he keeps his head down, and hopes the explosions happen some-where else.

Estelle was muttering now, and practically climbing in the mirror, doing something with her face. I couldn't work out what she was saying at all. Neither could Dad. He had to ask her to repeat herself. This time it came out as a giant snarl.

'It's not *my* fault if you don't listen!'

Dad sighed. I started a sigh count. That was two.

'We do listen to you, Estelle. It's just that neither your mother nor myself remembers hearing you say anything at all about needing six pounds for a field trip.'

He spoke for both of them because Mum had pulled the downie up over her head. She was just a long green lump in the bed now, like a body bag in some American war film. Mum can't stand arguments early in the morning. She's a lawyer, so she gets them from the moment she steps in the office. Before nine, she hands them straight over to Dad the same way William Saffery used to hand his rifle over to his friend Chalky whenever he saw someone in the enemy trenches exposed to fire too early in the day. He couldn't bear to start off his morning by killing a man. And I can understand that.

Estelle was still rubbing Mum's very expensive black make-up stick round and round her eyes.

'I suppose you think I'm lying!'

Dad sighed again. (Three.)

'That's not very nice, Estelle. And it's not fair. I don't believe you're lying. I'd just like you to have the good manners to tell me a little bit about this field trip before I dip in my wallet to pay for it.'

Estelle's so clever, the way she twists things round.

'You *hate* spending money on anything to do with me, don't you? You'll buy things for the others. You bought Muffy a whole bed last week—'

'Estelle, Muffy can't sleep in a cot bed *for ever*.'

'And you bought Will that calculator!'

'He's taking *maths*, Estelle!'

'And all I do is ask you for six miserable pounds to go with the rest of my class to Sanderley Tree Park, and you end up giving me a giant great row!'

There were some funny noises coming up from Mum's side of the bedclothes. At first I thought that they were just more sighs. But then I realized she was going apoplectic. Quick as he could, Dad moved his leg across, to pin her down. And by the time she'd managed to tear the covers off, to get at Estelle, he'd slid his arm round the back of her head, and clapped his great big hand over her mouth. Mum put up a really good fight. It must have taken a lot of strength to keep her down. If he'd let go suddenly, I wouldn't have been the slightest bit surprised to see Mum shoot up and crack her head on the ceiling.

And then Estelle turned round. It was incredible. She'd put such lashings of Mum's precious black stuff round her eyes, she looked like a raccoon.

Mum went demented. Dad could hardly keep her pinned to the bed while Estelle sailed off towards the door.

'It's quite all right,' she said. (The Martyr Queen.) 'I needn't go. All I have to do is tell Miss Sullivan that you won't pay for it . . .'

That one got straight through to Dad. Instantly he was out of bed and on his feet. Released, Mum started howling at Estelle's departing back: 'Don't you *dare* tell Miss Sullivan any such thing!' Dad grabbed his jacket and upended it. Everything in his pockets spilled out, and a handful of coins rolled away on the carpet. He snatched them up and, rushing past Muffy, who had just appeared in her pyjamas at the doorway, he flung them as hard as he could down the stairs after Estelle.

'Go on your bloody field trip!' he shouted. 'Don't let us stop you! Go out in the country and have a nice time kicking blackbirds and spitting at the rabbits!'

Muffy looked horrified. The front door banged. The house shook. Then there was silence. William Scott Saffery says there is no silence like the silence after an attack. It has a quality, he says, so real you can reach out and touch it. It's like that sometimes after Estelle goes. We wait quietly together. Muffy climbs into the bed, but nobody speaks. And then, at last, Mum and Dad eye one another as they hear the click of the front gate. Cease-fire! Mum sinks back against the pillows, her face white. Sometimes her hands are shaking so badly she can't even hold the teacup Dad offers her. She has to put it down and have a good cry.

Sighing (Four? Five? In the heat of the battle I'd entirely lost count), Dad rooted through his pockets and then through Mum's handbag, and held out the results of his search: one twenty-pound note and twenty-seven pence.

We're not allowed to take large banknotes to school.

'It's all right,' I told him. 'It doesn't matter. I'll make myself a sandwich.'

'You're a good lad, Will.'

Mum couldn't speak. She just gave me a little nod as I leaned over and kissed her goodbye. It takes her hours to get over Estelle.

* * *

There wasn't anything in the fridge, of course. All I could find was a heel of stale bread and two rather shrivelled carrots. I made a stale carrot sandwich. It wasn't very nice. Even Chopper raised his eyebrows when he saw it, and he hasn't won any prizes recently for bringing nutritious and appetizing sandwich combinations into the school lunch hall. We sat together at the paupers' table, and watched my sister sail past carrying a plate piled high with chips and salad and pizza.

I did my imitation of the last reel of *Exorcist IV*. Tipping my chair back, I flattened myself against the wall in mock terror, and held up my fingers in the shape of a cross.

I croaked out in hoarse, broken whispers:

'See that thing there, Chopper? It *looks* right, doesn't it? And it *sounds* right. It even *walks* right. But beware, Chopper! Beware! That thing there is *not my sister!*'

At my side, Chopper slid down in his chair so far he was practically under the table. All you could see were the whites of his eyes.

''Tis the Banshee of Beechcroft Avenue!' His voice grated over the words like feet over gravel

35

in a graveyard. 'Those who do hear her wail by day lay cold as stones by nightfall!'

'Cover your ears!'

'And watch her floating by, pale wraith of Death, pulling her cloak around her bony shoulders like a shroud.'

We'd learned it all from one of the books I'd picked up for Muffy at a branch library sale: *Tales of the Unnatural*. Mum wouldn't let me read it to Muffy, so I read it to Chopper instead. He'd liked the bit about the Banshee best. But since he couldn't remember any more, now he just took one last forlorn look across the room at Estelle, and finished up sadly:

'She always *used* to be all right. She was good fun, in fact. She let me run the bank in Monopoly, even though I get muddled.'

'She used to lend me her skateboard even when she wanted it herself. Now she hasn't touched it for a year, but if I so much as lay a foot on it, she flies out of her cage.'

'She spat tintacks at me yesterday when I called her Stelly.'

I was horrified. 'You never dared call her Stelly!'

He turned a wistful look on me. 'We *used* to be able to call her Stelly.'

I poked my horrible sandwich. 'She *used* to be all right.'

Now Chopper's wistful look seemed to have redirected itself towards my plate. 'Are you eating that thing?' he asked me. 'Because, if you're not, I'll swap it for the rest of this yoghurt. I think it's gone off.'

I nodded after Estelle.

'I expect that's because she walked past it.'

His eyes followed mine. Estelle was sitting with a pack of her mates. (Miss Adulewebe used to call them The Coven.) When they saw Chopper and me watching, they stuck out their tongues. Flora's was covered with cottage cheese.

Chopper picked up what was left of my carrot sandwich. I dipped a finger in his yoghurt pot. It tasted perfectly all right to me.

'I'm writing a book about what's going on at our house,' I confessed suddenly. 'What I intend to do is set down the whole grim and appalling story exactly as it happens.'

Chopper turned and stared. I realized that, without thinking, I had used William Scott Saffery's stiff and old-fashioned turn of phrase.

And then, by the strangest coincidence, Chopper responded with the very same words as

Chalky, when William finally explained to him exactly what it was he was so determinedly scribbling in all the quiet times between attacks.

'Why waste your time, Will? After all, you'll never get to finish it.'

Chapter 3

I will, though. I know I will. In our very first lesson with Miss Adulewebe, she told us the secret of writing anything. 'Get your bum on your seat.' Everyone argued, but she was adamant. 'Honestly. That is the hardest part. Sit down and pick up your pen, and after that it's downhill all the way.' She said it with perfect confidence that morning, though I admit she never said it again. I don't think Marisa's silly giggling put her off so much as the fact that, once she'd read some of Chopper's written work, she didn't believe it any longer. She'd bitten dust.

Poor Chopper just can't write. He has no problem speaking. Words tend to come out of his mouth in a sensible order. But ask him to write them down, and what you get is some thick claggy mess that goes round and round, but never reaches a full stop. None of it makes any sense.

'I can't read this,' Miss Adulewebe said, when he handed in his first effort.

Chopper just sighed. He tried to comfort her the same way he comforts other teachers. 'Never mind, miss. Perhaps it will be better when Will's helped me turn it into English.'

She turned and scowled. I think she thought he was joking. She didn't know that that's how we've been going on ever since Mr Astley took a major fit after struggling through Chopper's desperate account of five main climate types. ('You've *crucified* my subject, Chopperly! *Crucified* it!') Chopper was terribly hurt. He sulked till the end of the lesson, when Mr Astley ambled over to apologize and offer him one of his peppermints. Then he cheered up. But after that, Chopper almost always asked me to go through his home-work for him. I didn't mind. He's a good friend. And I don't get in any trouble. Everyone who teaches Chopper knows that he and the untangled paragraph are all but perfect strangers. At least with me scorching through his written work first, they get a clearer run. It isn't cheating, since they mark him down.

But till Miss Adulewebe came along, no one

had been insensitive enough to make remarks about the way we operate. She tipped the apple-cart over. She made us do a timed exercise under her nose: ten study questions on *To Kill A Mockingbird*. I chummed Chopper through the first seven, but then I had to leave early for the dentist just as Miss Adulewebe said, 'Ten minutes more!'

Like a fool, Chopper finished it.

It came back a few days later, dropped from a great height onto our double desk. Unnerved, Chopper made the mistake of asking,

'How was it?'

Miss Adulewebe looked us up and down and said with withering scorn:

'To the extent that it was written by Will here, it was all right, I suppose. To the extent that it was written by you, Chopper, it was irredeemably frightful.'

No, she didn't mince words, Miss Adulewebe. Still, I liked her lessons. Never again was she rash enough to claim that all there was to writing was getting your bum on a seat and picking up your pencil, but she did deal out reams of other advice. She warned Stormer Phillips as early as the third week of term that if he was ill-advised enough to give her one more piece of written work stuffed with his brainless comic-speak ('Pow!' 'Bang!' 'Yipes!' 'Aaaargh!') she'd personally rip his ears off. She told Marisa that if she ever again ended an essay with the words 'And then I woke up and found it was all a dream', she'd find herself on the floor. And she was mighty rude to me, always flapping my essays around my ears before she gave them back.

'You shouldn't be sitting next to Chopper. It makes you smug and lazy.'

No, Miss Adulewebe didn't have much patience. I think that's why she left. Scotbags made me lug some of her stuff out to her car on the last day. ('You're a hulking great lad, Flowers! Carry Miss Adulewebe's boxes for her. Jump to it!')

She turned from stowing everything away neatly on the back seat. 'Oh, it's you. Good. I have something to say to you.'

It sounded a bit threatening.

'What have *I* done?'

She drew herself up, leaned against the car door, and gave me a good long look.

'I'll tell you your problem, Will Flowers. You write things down all right, but then you always take very great care to leave out what you *feel*.

Keep on like that, and everything you ever write will be entirely bloodless.'

Charming. I carry her boxes for her. She puts a curse on me.

Chopper sidled up just as the car shot off, spurting out clouds of black oil fumes.

'What was all that about?'

'Nothing.'

But it stuck in my mind. And, naturally, now I've decided to write a whole book, I worry she might be right, and I'm not saying enough about how I feel when 27 Beechcroft Avenue gets turned upside down by my ferocious sister rattling her cage bars. But it's not easy. Often I don't know. I am a bit like poor Muffy when she ends up in the no man's land of the middle of the carpet just as Estelle decides it's a good time to fire a shot or two at Mum and Dad.

'Alison's having a party on Friday night and I've said I'm going. That's all right, isn't it?'

Muffy's eyes widen. Since she adores Estelle, part of her wants to climb in her lap just as she always has when anything makes her unhappy or nervous. But the rest of her wants to run for cover. And so she's torn. The poor thing ends up standing there paralysed in her yellow bedtime gnome suit with the built-in feet, sucking her thumb harder and harder as things hot up.

'Which Alison is this, Estelle?'

'Will her parents be there?'

'What time will it finish?'

Sometimes there is an unexpected break in fire. 'I think I remember Alison! Wasn't she that nice girl we met once at the swimming pool? She looked rather sensible.' And Muffy's eyes light up. Maybe she even feels brave enough to shuffle over and lean against Estelle's end of the sofa. But before long the argument is raging again.

'It's not *fair*! I'm not a baby like Muffy! Why can't I go?'

Muffy's face falls. The most she'll manage now is to uncork her thumb just long enough to plead: 'Not a game, Stelly! Not a game!'

And who thinks it's a game? Certainly not Estelle. You'd think, to hear her, that one of her ambitions all life long had been to go to Alison's party. And certainly *I* don't. I realize straight away it's curtains for my chances of getting any help from anyone with my French before tomorrow's test. And Mum and Dad get furious with Estelle for setting off these grinding barrage attacks, day after day, about what she can wear and where she can go, and what time she has to be back again.

Mum takes Estelle aside time and again.

'You listen to me, young lady. You had a peaceable enough time when you were Muffy's age. Why should your sister have to grow up forever listening to you fighting your battles? What sort of childhood is that? Why can't you show a bit of self-control?'

And she might even try. But it won't last. Hardly an hour goes by, and she is off again.

'I don't see why I can't go to this party. Everyone else is going. And one o'clock isn't all that late.'

This time it's Dad's turn to try and spike her guns.

'For heaven's sake, Estelle! Can't we get peacefully through one single meal? Remember what your mother said. This isn't fair on Muffy.'

'Muffy!' Her voice brims with scorn. 'Muffy's all right.' She turns to her. '*Aren't* you?'

Beaming, Muffy nods.

'See!' triumphs Estelle. 'She's all right. She doesn't mind.'

Mum didn't say anything, but I saw her glancing anxiously at Dad, and I knew what she was thinking. Dr Rombauer at the clinic insists that it's just a stage Muffy's going through, hardly ever speaking. She'll soon grow out of it and 'make with the words', as he puts it. But Mum sometimes worries that, with all the endless wrangling in the house, Muffy might stay silent for ever.

Unlike Estelle. She was off on another tack.

'And I don't see why I have to go round never saying what I think, and not standing up for myself, just so Muffy can grow up in some fairy tale!'

Dad sighs. 'There's nothing fairy-tale about wanting a little bit of peace and quiet during a meal . . .'

'There is if you live in—'

I block my ears, so I don't have to listen. Muffy might not mind, but I do. I've heard Estelle too often before, reeling off the names of one war-torn country after another. Now I've read *The Longest Summer*, I hate to be reminded that there are boys the same age as William Saffery and myself toting their guns in all the places on her dreadful list. I didn't stop pressing my fingers in my ears until I thought I was safe because I saw Dad was speaking.

It was a pity that the first remark he made was

that she should drop the whole subject till after we'd finished our meal.

Mistake! Mistake! That simply set Estelle off about how lucky we all were to be eating at all. Muffy looked down at her bacon pie, mystified. And before anybody could step in, Estelle set about explaining to Muffy how there were others our age all over the world, starving in famines and slums and refugee camps because people like Mum and Dad were so busy stuffing bacon pie down the throats of their own families, they had no time to think about other people's children.

Mum lost her temper.

'That's enough, Estelle!'

(Mum hates to cook, so if there's one thing she can't stand at meals, it's base ingratitude.)

Estelle went quiet, and started to shunt her food moodily around her plate, making a point of not taking any mouthfuls. The poison of her mood rolled over the table like a cloud of gas, but unlike William Saffery in his trench, we hadn't been issued with masks so we had no protection. First Muffy's spoon drifted to a halt. She couldn't eat for worrying about Estelle not finishing her supper. Dad raised his eyes to heaven and laid down his fork. Without thinking, I stopped too, waiting to see what happened.

Determinedly, Mum kept on swallowing. But you could tell from the look on her face that each mouthful tasted more like cardboard than the last.

In the end even she gave up, and pushed her food away.

'Well done, Estelle,' she said. 'Another meal ruined.'

Estelle was furious.

'That's right! Blame me! Of course, it has to be *my* fault.'

Slamming her knife and fork down, she flounced out, banging the door hard behind her. In the silence that followed, Dad swivelled round to face Muffy. Stretching a finger out, he caught one of her fat shiny tears just as it brimmed over to roll down her cheek.

'Pudding,' he said, inspecting it closely and smacking his lips. 'Yum, yum!'

Muffy brightened. The tear on the other cheek rolled down and away, but no more welled up in her eyes to replace them. Dad turned the other way, to Mum, patting her hand on the table. Putting on a fruity old-fashioned army brigadier's voice, he said to her:

'That's War for you, my darling.' Thrusting his jaw out, he stared across the room. 'And War is Hell . . .'

Mum wasn't in the mood. She nodded angrily towards the door.

'I'll tell you that young lady's problem. She doesn't know who her friends are. Will is enough of a pain—'

I glanced up in surprise. Oh, yes? How come it's Estelle who flounces out, but suddenly we're talking about me?

'—blaring that frightful music out of his room night and day, and sticking those horrible posters all over his nice honeysuckle wallpaper. Disappearing into his bedroom at the first sign of having to pitch in with the housework—'

'Excuse me!' I broke in. 'I am still sitting here. Alive. With two ears that work.'

More than hers did, I can tell you. She just kept on.

'Will's bad enough, forever shambling about like something Frankenstein knocked up at night. Bursting through doors without bothering to stop and turn the handle. Picking the leaves off every houseplant he walks past. Chewing his bus tickets so half the time he ends up paying twice—'

I'd given up. I simply sat staring as she poured out this catalogue of failings I hadn't even known I had.

'Getting in all those stupid fights with Stormer Phillips on the way home from school, and setting fire to next-door's shed like that, and saying, "Eh?" like a halfwit whenever anybody speaks to him—'

'Steady on, old girl!'

(Brigadier Flowers getting it together at last.)

But it was too late. She'd almost finished with me anyway.

'Will is enough of a pain. But Estelle!' She leaned across the table. Her sleeve fell in the bacon pie, but she didn't notice. 'We do our best, and she just treats us like enemies. At least Will's not like that. At least he's always known who's on his side.'

She turned to me.

'*Haven't* you?' she demanded, just the way Estelle speaks to Muffy.

Like Muffy, I couldn't help beaming and nodding. But I was not so sure. I don't know who's on whose side. This isn't war. Mind you, sometimes I think it might be a whole lot simpler if we went round in different coloured uniforms to show where our sympathies lay in each particular battle. 'Oh, look. She's one of us today. She's wearing khaki.' 'Watch out for him. He's just gone up to change back into field grey.'

But it probably wouldn't work. Even William Scott Saffery had problems working out who was the enemy. As I helped Mum and Dad clear the table, I thought about the time he was scrambling back from a night raid and a shell fell so close it blasted him out of his senses. He crawled off, bleeding steadily, the wrong way through no man's land, but the sweep of a machine gun over the field of mud and wire soon sent him hurtling into the safety of a shell hole. A flare shot up and fell in an arc of livid green. In its brief light, he watched bullets flying over the lip of the hole. *Rat-a-tat-tat-tat-tat-tat!* Then suddenly into his private swamp of mud and blood fell someone else in desperate need of shelter. Whoever it was landed heavy as a saddlebag. As William rolled to face this new danger, another flare shot up. The bilious light hung for its few long moments in the sky, and William and the other boy looked gravely at one another. Then, with no words, the two of them came to an understanding. Gently, so as not to startle someone no older than himself into a deadly mistake, the boy lifted his arm, and pointed out the true direction of William's front line. In return, William drew back his bayonet.

Will got back safely. That night, he says, he hoped aloud to God the other boy did too. 'I felt no enmity,' he wrote. 'Why should I? Without the dying splutter of the flare, how would I even have known that, where mud and blood had failed to cover it, his uniform was not, like mine, khaki, but the dreaded field grey?'

And that's how I feel about Estelle. She doesn't chew Mum's plants, or burn down sheds. She even opens door quietly. (Makes up for that, of course, the way she slams them shut.) She doesn't say '*Eh?*' and no one would ever call her an idiot. (They wouldn't dare.) She doesn't get on their nerves in exactly the same ways as I do. She has her own style. But that doesn't make her my enemy. And sometimes I even think Estelle has right on her side. You take the row at supper. Was what she said so terrible? Was it so wrong? We all watch television. We see the news. We know all about the children she's describing to Muffy. We've seen them staring through the netting of their camps, or wasting away on their mats. Maybe Estelle is right, and we shouldn't sit filling our faces with pie day after day, not even talking about them because it's 'rude'.

But then sometimes I think she's wrong. She's got the wrong end of the stick. It's not that Mum and Dad don't care about horrible things. I know they do. I've heard Mum often enough, when Dad leans forward to change television channels. 'Oh, no, George. Not the news. Not tonight, please. I couldn't stand it.'

That's not indifference. That's simply having had enough.

And what's the point of going on and on about terrible things, if you can't stop them? Mum's not the only person in the world who wants to blot them out. Last week, when Gran borrowed me and Estelle to shift some furniture around in her bedroom, we came across an old cardboard dress box full of photographs at the bottom of the wardrobe. Estelle picked out one of five fancy ladies sitting on a bench at the seaside, dressed up as if they were about to go to church. In front of them, stabbing the sand with a little wooden spade, was someone the same age as Muffy. We couldn't tell if it was a boy or a girl.

'Who's this?'

Gran took a look.

'That's my grandmother.'

'*Yours?*'

Gran gave Estelle a warning look.

'People my age didn't come out of tins,' she said tartly.

'And who are all the ladies?'

'My great-grandmother and her four sisters.' She pointed one by one along the line. 'Rose, Elsie, Greta, Matty and Daisy.'

Estelle rooted in the box. A few layers down, she found what was almost the same photo over again. There was the same wide line of white hotels facing the sands, the same tall lampstands curving over the promenade. But, this time, the child on the beach was old enough to have built a sandcastle with a wide foaming moat and four magnificent turrets.

And this time the sisters were all dressed in black.

'Everyone was in mourning by then,' explained Gran. 'It was such a terrible war!' She stroked the photo and a memory came back. 'Do you know, my grandmother told me once that when she ran down to the beach on their first holiday after the war, she couldn't understand why the sea sounded so different. She asked her mother,

"Where's that other noise?" and Rose glanced at her sisters. "What other noise, dear?" said Aunty Matty. "The waves sound just the same, surely." But my grandmother persisted. "Yes, the waves sound the same. But where's the noise you told me was the huge rocks on the sea bed, rolling and banging against one another?" One by one, the aunts looked away uneasily and wouldn't answer her. And Grandmother realized for the very first time that, during all those endless summer days spent on the beach, what she'd been hearing was the guns in France.'

I felt quite sick. Gran handed me the photograph to put back in the box, and I couldn't even bear to glance at it again, knowing that, summer after long summer those sisters had sat in a row and listened to the guns that were killing their husbands and brothers and uncles, and said nothing in front of the children.

'Didn't they *care*?' Estelle demanded.

'Of course they cared,' Gran replied. 'People with self-control don't have any fewer feelings. They felt the same as anyone else when they were handed their black-edged telegrams.'

'But not to say!'

Gran shrugged.

'Stiff upper lip.'

Estelle went mad.

'Fools!' she yelled. 'Idiots! Couldn't they *see* it was a waste? Didn't they *realize* that it was self-control like theirs that let that horrible war go on for years?'

Gran didn't argue with her. Neither did I. Perhaps Estelle's right, and people should speak up more. There is a bit in William Saffery's book when he leans back in a ditch and lets himself daydream about what he would say if he had the chance to show the Big Brass round the battle-field. He'd tell them what he thought of their great 'war to end all wars'. His words burn off the page, and I can hear behind his scorching sarcasms, his bitter wit, the scathing tones of Estelle. Though he probably died of old age before she was born, and she's not read his book, the two of them have a lot in common. Neither would trade a child's unruffled summers on the beach for nothing said about the war in France.

In fact, sometimes, late at night, I get confused. I put down the book and lie in the dark, thinking about what I've read, and an image swims up in front of me. I see the slight young body in the uniform, the tousled hair. But it's Estelle's face I see, though it's a boy's face. And when his withering descriptions of all the horrors he sees around ring in my head, it's Estelle's voice I hear.

And that's not surprising. Some of the things they say sound so alike. But he stayed in the war month after month. Oh, he wrote his doubts down secretly when he could; but he kept shooting at those other boys, not very much older than himself. Estelle would never have done that. She would have flung her rifle in a ditch, rather than be a part of anything about which she had so many doubts.

Who's braver? Who cares more?

I'm more like William, I know. I'd see it through. Whether you kick up a storm about something is really a matter of the way you are, or the way you've been brought up. It doesn't prove what you feel. Surely it's only chance – like the colour of the uniform you end up wearing if you're about my age when war starts up, or the colour of ink you happen to have in your pen the day you start writing a book about your sister.

So I'm not going to worry any more about The Curse of Miss Adulewebe. Teachers aren't always right. If I don't choose to litter this book with my feelings, that's my affair. It could still be a good book. William Scott Saffery didn't go on and on about what he felt all the time. He simply set down what he saw – simple as that. He turned himself into the eyes and ears of war, and grimly and determinedly wrote it down, every last horror, exactly as it happened.

The Impeccable War Reporter.

That'll be me.

Chapter 4

Friday 29th September. 07.52 hours. *Dawn Attack!*

Dad was the first to sense danger. As usual I was up and dressed, and standing at the end of their bed, rooting through pockets in search of lunch money. Mum couldn't be seen at all. She was under the downie. Dad's head was on the pillow, his eyes closed. I thought he was clinging to the last shreds of sleep, but suddenly his eyes snapped open. I froze. I wondered for a moment if he was going to tell me off. Had I picked a leaf off the geranium without thinking? Had I barged through the door like something Dr Frankenstein knocked up at night? But no. He wasn't looking at me. He was staring up at the ceiling. And when he spoke, it was in the clipped tones of the experienced military officer, Leader of Men:

'It's too quiet out there. I don't like it.'

Mum didn't stir.

Dad went on in hushed and urgent whispers in spite of the fact that, hidden underneath her downie mound, Mum obviously couldn't hear a word.

'It was like this once before, Flowers. Do you remember? Silent as armistice morning. We could hear nothing out there. Nothing. No bleating about lost school books. No squabbling over the last few coins for lunch money. No moaning about how long other people were hogging the bathroom. Then, suddenly – do you remember? All hell let loose! They hurled everything they had at us!' He threw himself under the downie. *'Dawn attack!'*

The door burst open. But it was only Muffy. She padded over in her little yellow gnome suit and stood beside the bed, looking at both lumps of downie. Then she poked the side that was Dad.

'Stelly's not going,' she told it.

Part of the downie flinched. A muffled voice came out from a fortified bulge.

'Not going where?'

'School.'

'Ah . . .'

There was no further response, though Muffy waited a while, watching the bed, in case one or another of the lumps heaved into life. But when after a couple of minutes nothing had happened, she turned and padded back to the door.

As soon as it clicked behind her, the bedclothes flew down, and Brigadier Flowers took up his War Memoirs.

'We'd faced this sort of attack before, of course. We called it "The Banshee" because it seemed to come out of nowhere with no warning, an ominous portent of impending doom—'

Mum pushed back her side of the downie.

'Are you *getting* up, George? Or do I have to go down and sort everyone out before I get dressed for work?'

Dad looked quite horrified.

'No, no!' he said. 'You stay here. It's far safer!'

He swung his legs over the side of the bed, and reached for his dressing gown. Mum fell back in the bed. Dad turned to me.

'Right, lad,' he said, handing me last night's tea tray. 'Watch my back. I'm going down there to face your sister. I want steady covering fire.'

'Could I have some lunch money?'

He brushed me aside.

'Later, lad. Later. Can't you see there's a war on?'

'Mu-*um*?'

She pulled the downie over her head, and groaned.

I followed Dad out of the room.

'I had a piccalilli sandwich yesterday,' I told him. 'The day before that, I had to have mint sauce on crackers. I need some lunch money, Dad. I want proper food.'

'Ssshh, lad. Keep your voice down.'

He was creeping along the landing. As he drew level with the bathroom door, he drew himself up and banged on its panels.

'Hurry along in there!' he shouted. 'There are other people waiting!'

Just at that moment Muffy padded up, looked at him as if he were mad, pushed the bathroom door open and went in. It had been empty.

Dad crept on down the stairs, making the banisters take his weight so there were fewer warning creaks.

'Da-*ad*—'

He wasn't listening. Outside the kitchen door he paused to brace himself. Then he threw open the door. Estelle was sprawled at the table, still wearing her dressing gown and slippers. Her hair was a rat's nest. Beside her, a mug sat in a little pool of spilled coffee, some of which was soaking up her sleeve. She didn't care. She was idly painting her nails green and reading a pop magazine that was propped up against a milk carton. On its cover was a photograph of the lead singer of the Black Plague Rats, leaping up out of a sewer and waving his guitar.

'Morning, Estelle,' said Dad.

She lifted her head and scowled at him.

'I'm not going,' she announced. 'I told Muffy to tell you. I'm not going to school.'

Dad took the tray from me and put it down on the draining board. Deftly, he refilled the kettle, plugged it in, and slid the dirty cups off the tea tray.

'You have to go to school, dear,' he told her. 'It's the law.'

'Then the law's stupid,' Estelle said.

Dad reached up for the tea caddy.

'And so will you be, dear, if you don't go.'

I grinned. (I couldn't help it.) Estelle turned and caught me at it. She shot me such a poisonous look that when Dad glanced in her direction, he went pale. And he only caught the tail end of it.

'More coffee?' he asked her as brightly as he could.

Her face went black.

'No.'

Dad's bright tone took on a bit of a steely edge.

'No, *what*, Estelle?'

'No, *thank* you,' she said with real venom.

'That's better, dear.' He turned back to the kettle. 'Now tell me what's bothering you,' he said, and it was only because I came up behind him to get the cornflake packet out of the corner cupboard that I heard him adding quietly, under his breath: 'You miserable, bad-tempered old maggot.'

Estelle must have caught something.

'What did you say?'

He didn't dare repeat it.

'I said tell Daddy why you don't feel like going to school today.'

Estelle tried to push her hair back impatiently, in one of those film-star gestures she picks up off Flora. But it was so long since she'd brushed it properly, her hand got caught in the tangles.

'It's not that I don't *feel* like it. I'm just not going. It's a waste of time. I've gone for years and

64

years and years, and I'm not going any longer. I've had enough.'

Dad heaped Mum's crunchy granola into a bowl on the tea tray.

'You have to go to school, Estelle,' he said. 'It's education, you see. Education. It's what distinguishes Man—'

Proudly, he threw his chest out and pointed to himself. Then he snatched up her magazine, and pointed to the lead singer of the Black Plague Rats.

'— from Animal.'

Estelle snatched the magazine back.

'Not in our school, it isn't! We don't do anything worth doing. We never get to learn anything. Nobody ever listens. We never do anything interesting. And, if we do, Mark Hanley and Rich Sheens muck about all the time, and ruin it. So I'm not going. It's just a cosmic waste of time.'

I thought she had a point. Dad didn't, though.

'It can't *all* be a waste of time, Estelle. You must have learned *something* over the years. You can *read*, can't you?'

Estelle went back to her nails.

'Mum says she taught me to read. It wasn't

school. She says if Miss Philomena had her way, I'd still be staring at non-sexist, non-racist, non-classist work sheets, unable to decipher a single word. She says she had to go round to Gran and dig out all her old *Janet and John* books. Then I could read in a week.'

Dad was trying very hard to pretend he wasn't hearing this.

'And you can *write*.'

Estelle was outraged.

'I like that! What a cheek! You're *always* on at me about my writing!'

Dad made the mistake of persisting.

'And you *know* things! You know where France and Russia are – oh, no. You don't know where they are, do you? That came up only yesterday . . .'

Estelle moved in for the kill.

'See? *See?* You *know* it's useless! You and Mum have been going on about how useless it is for years and years.' She made the bilious green fingernails of one hand chatter to the nails of the other, imitating Mum and Dad having one of their five million conversations a week about the sorry state of affairs at Wallace Secondary School. '"What does she *do* all day, that's what I'd like to know." "Well, she certainly doesn't seem to learn anything." "That's true. Do you know, I found out today that she doesn't even have the faintest idea where Russia is. Russia!" "That doesn't surprise me in the slightest. I don't think they teach them anything. I don't think they even bother to look at their work." "They most certainly don't bother to correct it!" '

It was a pretty good imitation. Dad looked embarrassed.

Estelle put the boot in properly as she picked up her bottle of nail polish, and drifted towards the door.

'You and Mum can't have it both ways. Ever since I first started at that school, you two have been going on about what a waste of time it is, and how little I learn. Now I'm *agreeing* with you! And you *still* want to shovel me out of the door! How hypocritical!'

Again, I thought she had a point. Dad didn't, though.

'Hypocritical or not, you have to go to school.'

'I don't.'

'You do.'

'No, I *don't*!'

BANG!

Dad didn't let himself get rattled under fire.

Calmly he poured fresh tea into the mugs, picked up the tray and strode over to the door, standing in front of it until I thought to reach out and pull it open. Then he walked through.

Still desperate for lunch money, I snatched up my bowl of cornflakes and followed him up the stairs. As he neared the bathroom, he slid the weight of the tray onto one hand, and beat on the panels of the door with the other.

'Hurry along in there, please! There are other people waiting.'

The door opened. Mum's arm reached out and lifted a mug off the tray as it passed by. I trailed in after it, like someone following the Holy Grail, and sat on the edge of the bath with my cornflakes.

'Mum—'

She wasn't listening. There was someone else on her mind. In between lipsticking and eyelash blackening, she called out:

'How's it going, George?'

He showed up in the doorway.

'It's not. I mean, she's not. She says school's just a cosmic waste of time.'

Mum gave herself a little 'so tell me something new' shrug in the mirror. 'She's right there.'

'And she says she doesn't learn anything.'

'No more she does,' agreed Mum.

'And when they do something interesting, which isn't very often, Mark Hanley and Rich Sheens always muck about and spoil it.'

'Right.' Mum nodded. She'd heard that often enough before.

'So she's not going.'

Mum took a fit.

'Oh yes, she is! She's certainly not staying home all day. I'd go mad!'

'You're out at work.'

'Well, *you*'d go mad.'

'But I'm out at work too.'

Mum tugged her jacket on, and buttoned it up.

'Then that settles it, doesn't it?' she said firmly. 'She certainly can't spend the whole day in the house by herself.' She turned and made for the banisters. 'Estelle! You just get dress—'

She never got any further. Dad sprang on her from behind. Clapping his hand over her mouth, he pulled her away from the banisters.

'Sssh!' he hissed. 'Stop it! Don't draw her fire! Give us a minute to re-group. Re-arm. Get dressed.'

Still covering her mouth, he hauled her back with him, into the bedroom.

I followed them.

'About my lunch money—'

Neither of them was listening. He was rooting through drawers and cupboards, throwing on clothes as fast as he could. She was checking the papers in her briefcase. Then she looked up and noticed me for the first time since 07:52 hours. (It was now 08:07.)

'I do wish you wouldn't walk about the house eating,' she told me. 'Go downstairs at once, and finish those cornflakes in the kitchen.'

I didn't argue. Since it was obvious I wasn't going to get a proper lunch, I thought I'd better have another breakfast anyway. Downstairs, Muffy was dressed and sitting at the table, spooning granola from her china rabbit bowl. I took the seat beside her and poured myself another round of cornflakes. She shunted the milk towards me, and we ate in companionable silence till she tipped her bowl for the final spoonful of milk, and revealed the three bunnies that spend their rather risky china lives scampering around the bottom. Seeing them reminded me of when I took a short cut back from next door over our rabbit hutch and, hearing a sob from inside it, looked in to find Muffy sitting all squashed up under the netting roof, squeezing poor Thumper till his eyes were nearly popping out of his head, and weeping noisily into his fur.

'What's going on here?' I'd demanded.

She didn't speak. She just wiped a slug trail off her nose onto Thumper, and looked up with brimming eyes.

'Come on, now, Muff,' I said. 'If you don't tell me what's wrong, how can I sort it out?'

She did it for Thumper, you could tell.

'Stelly!' she said.

I prodded her along a bit.

'Did Stelly do something to Thumper?'

She shook her head, and squeezed him even more tightly. Hastily I said:

'Did she say something, then?'

Muffy nodded. Her mop of hair shook violently.

'Make with the words, Muffy,' I said impatiently. 'What did she say?'

'Stelly said she was going to cook him!' wailed Muffy.

For heaven's sake! I'd put her right on that. I dried her tears. I prised poor Thumper safely out of her grasp, and settled him down on his straw. Then, out of curiosity, I'd asked Muffy:

'Tell me, can you remember how things used to be?'

She didn't answer, but I knew she was listening hard.

'What I *mean*,' I said, picking my words carefully. 'What I mean is, can you remember what things were like in this house before Estelle went all funny?'

She gave me a look. It was impenetrable, but since she'd used up her word hoard for the day filling me in on Estelle's culinary threats, I didn't press her. I just carried on.

'If you remember,' I told her, 'things used to be very different. We all got up and lived our lives peacefully, and then went to bed again. There was none of all this—' I hesitated. 'All this—'

I couldn't think of a word. William Scott Saffery had that trouble once when the sun shot out cleanly from behind a cloud and flashed on the metal of his gun, dazzling him for a moment and making him see the hell's wilderness around him with a fresh eye, and wonder what sort of force it was that could make so many million men vie with one another to make their world such a shambles. What was the *name* of it? What was it *called*?

And I don't know the word either. But, like the great-aunts, I think someone Muffy's age should have a peaceful summer on a beach, and, like Mum, I don't want Muffy to grow up without some memories of pleasant breakfasts. So:

'Remember how it used to be,' I reminded her. 'Estelle used to sit in this seat next to you. I sat in the one over there across the table. And we had a race every morning to see who could empty their bowl first without being told off for gobbling.'

She smiled, so I knew she remembered. But she didn't speak. And something wistful in me made me spoil it all by adding bitterly:

'Now look at us. Estelle doesn't eat breakfast at all unless someone stands over her and watches. I've moved round to this seat. And the two of us don't bother to race because it's not so good without Stelly.'

Mistake!

'Don't call me Stelly!'

She'd slid through the door so quietly we hadn't heard. Muffy snatched up her spoon and pretended to be busy eating. She knew Estelle wasn't snapping at her. (Muffy is still excused from this particular page in Estelle's Book of Rules.) But she gets nervous when Estelle's in a mood.

I tried to draw the fire.

'You're still not dressed.'

'That's because I'm still not going.'

Muffy looked anxiously from one of us to the other. She may think the world of Estelle, but she does live here so she knows the rules. Unless you're dying, you are sent to school.

'She'll have to go,' I whispered, to stop Muffy worrying.

Estelle has ears on stalks.

'No, I won't.' She turned her back on us and started pouring boiling water into her coffee mug. 'They won't let me get my ears pierced like everyone else. So why should I go to school like everyone else? Fair's fair, after all.'

She had a point, I thought. But Muffy didn't.

'Got to get *dressed*, Stelly,' she warned, looking so anxious it would break your heart. 'Got to go to *school*.'

Mum came in just in time to hear the end of this. Her own way of telling Estelle what she ought to be doing may not have been quite so straightforward, but it came out a good deal more firmly.

'Goodness! Look at the time. It's after a quarter past eight already. Now hurry and put on some clothes, Estelle.'

You notice she didn't actually say, 'Get dressed for school.' Mum's like the gunner at the end of William Saffery's line, who learned exactly how often and how much he could spatter the enemy with machine-gun fire without provoking a great barrage back.

She judged it right, too. Estelle didn't flare up. She just muttered darkly into her coffee.

Mum pushed her luck.

'What was that, darling?'

'I haven't got anything to wear!' snapped Estelle.

I couldn't believe my ears. Nothing to wear? Estelle's wardrobe is groaning with clothes. You can't shut the door! Her floor's knee deep in them. She has all of her own clothes, half of mine, and several of Mum's that she's borrowed. Dad can never find any of his woollies. She's always got them too. I reckon, when it comes to clothes, Muffy's the only one round here who's halfway safe. I sat at the table with my mouth open. I was shocked. Nothing to wear indeed!

'You must have something, dear,' said Mum.

Estelle scowled.

'I *hate* my clothes. All of them. They're ugly and boring and stupid and out of date, and I've worn all of them a million times.'

'Once more won't matter, then, will it? Go up and put some on.'

'I'm not going to school in them,' Estelle warned her.

But Mum had suddenly had enough. She glanced at the clock. (08:21 hours.)

'Just go up and get dressed, Estelle! Before I lose my temper ...'

Slopping her coffee, Estelle flounced out. Mum sank down at the table for a moment, to gather herself together before the next round of fire. Muffy took to patting her. Mum patted Muffy back. The two of them were still patting one another when Dad peered round the door.

'Masterly!' he praised Mum. 'Masterly! A shrewd manoeuvre, Bridget. Once Estelle's dressed, the battle's practically won.'

'I've got a headache,' said Mum.

'Nonsense,' said Dad. 'This is no time to crack up. We have to work out the details of our plan of attack. Are we going to barricade the door against her, or let her back in for another argument?'

I thought I'd try one last time to get a look in. (I do live here too.)

'It takes her ages to get dressed,' I said. 'That gives you a bit of time to find me some lunch money.'

They only heard the first bit. It set them both off, looking at the clock.

'Twenty-five past!' cried Mum. 'It's nearly time for Muffy's car pool!'

Muffy slid off her chair, and went to fetch her jacket. She hates being late for the car pool.

Mum stood at the bottom of the stairs, listening.

'I can't hear a thing,' she said. 'It's absolutely silent up there.'

'That's Estelle dressing,' I said. Mum gave me a look, but I wasn't trying to be funny. I meant it. Some people are noisy dressers. Some people aren't. I'm quite loud myself. Every time I tug at my sock drawer it shoots out and lands on the floor. My cupboard door has to be slammed shut. And I often drop my shoes, or bang my head on my bookshelf. Estelle's much quieter. She floats around her room, trying a million things on, taking them off again, and silently dropping them on the floor.

'Who's going to hurry her up?' said Mum, mentioning no names but looking directly at Brigadier Flowers.

Like William Saffery's last company officer, Dad suddenly wasn't so keen to go over the top.

'You go.'

'No, you go.'

'You're her mother.'

'You're her father.'

Dad had an inspiration.

'Muffy can go.'

But Muffy had just seen a car pull up at the gate. Her face crumpled with worry.

'Got to go to *school* . . .'

Dad picked up her plastic Snoopy lunchbox and handed it to her as if it were a spotted handkerchief on a stick, and Muffy had just announced that she was going off to see the world.

'That's my Muffy!' he said proudly. 'There's my girl! Did you hear what she said, Bridget? "Got to go to school"! It's music to my ears. I'm proud of you, Muffy!'

He gave her a huge kiss and chummed her out

the door and down the path. (This wasn't anything special. He hasn't got round to taking the childproof lock off the gate yet, so Muffy always has to be chummed to the end of the garden.)

Mum used the time up staring at the clock.

'My God!' she said. 'It's twenty-five to nine!'

Dad came back fortified by a few lungfuls of fresh air and a word with Mrs Cuyugan, his favourite car-pool mother.

'Right, Bridget,' he ordered. 'The last push!' He put his hands on her shoulders and propelled her firmly through the door to the bottom of the stairs. 'You go first. I'll give you cover from behind.'

'While you're up there,' I said. 'Do you think you could borrow some cash off Estelle for my lunch money?'

But they weren't listening. They were busy going up the stairs. I say busy, because Mum kept clinging to the banisters, losing her nerve, and Dad had to keep sticking an imaginary gun in her back to keep her going.

Mum made an effort.

'Estelle! Are you ready yet? It's time to go, dear. If you hurry, Daddy can give you a lift as far as the garage. Estelle? Estelle . . . ?'

There was no answer. Mum moved up closer to Estelle's bedroom door, with Brigadier Flowers diligently bringing up the rear.

Mum pushed the door with a fingertip. It swung open. Together they peered in. I didn't need to come any further up to know what they were seeing. I've been in Estelle's room often enough, sifting through the mess to try and find things of mine. It's a dark tip. I once cut my toe on a tin of condensed milk, picking my way across to my best denim jacket through piles of abandoned woollies and her old tights droppings. Muffy's mouth organ was lost in here for a week, under a drift of knickers. And Dad says if she ever borrows any of his tools again and leaves them lying in her sink with the tap dripping, he'll personally bring his wrench down on what's left in her empty teenage skull, and cheerfully swing for it. But I was interested to see what Mum made of the sight. Usually she won't go near it. She says it's too upsetting and she can't stand it. It bothers her because, for hours afterwards, each time she looks at Muffy all she can think is: 'One day this child might go like this as well.'

So this was probably the first time for days that

she'd even glanced in Estelle's room. I came up close to watch. Her face went grim, and then it crumpled like Muffy's.

'Oh, it's horrible, George. Horrible!'

He tried to bury her head against his shoulder, so she wouldn't look at the details. I think he was worried she'd notice the stains on the wall where Estelle squidged her mauve *Paris Chic* spray glitter at me in a temper, or the bright rock-hard lumps on the surface of the dressing table where she and Flora propped the dripping brushes when they were varnishing their nails in coloured stripes.

'Shut your eyes,' he ordered her. 'Don't even think about it.'

She shuddered in his arms.

'I can't help it,' she said. 'I keep remembering how it used to be. Do you remember, George? Those sweet little bunny rabbit curtains blowing in the breeze. Cheerful posters on the walls. Furry toys on the bed. And everything was picked up off the floor every night.' She let out a little moan of anguish. 'Now look at it!'

He set his jaw like granite.

'A heap of smoking rubble . . .' he agreed.

Mum tried to twist out of his arms.

'It's all right. I don't want to look any more,' she assured him.

'Quite right. Best not to look.' He straightened his imaginary cap. 'Some day this senseless, senseless war will be over. Till then, let's just close the door and tiptoe quietly away . . .'

They got as far as the banisters. Then there was the most appalling noise from inside Estelle's room. It was extraordinary. It sounded as if the walls were caving in, one after another, and the ceiling was falling on top of them. It could just have been a shelf shearing away from its bracket, I suppose. But it sounded a lot worse than that. It sounded like an avalanche.

Mum and Dad clutched one another.

'What was *that*?'

'Quick, George!'

Dad pushed the door open again.

Mum was beside herself.

'What *is* it, George?'

He drew his head back, and shrugged.

'Hard to tell, Bridget. It looks just the same as it did before to me. Probably just a landslide. There's so much junk in there, you just can't tell. It was so messy anyway . . .'

Mum took one of her fits. Sometimes, you can

tell, the thought flashes through her mind that this house is half hers, and she's going to run it her way. Striding along to the bathroom, she rattled the handle like someone demented, then beat on the door with her fists.

'*Estelle! Estelle!* I don't care whether you've washed your face or cleaned your teeth. I don't even care what you're wearing. I just want you out of this bathroom in three seconds flat, and off to school out of my sight!'

She put her hands on her hips. She meant business.

'One!'

Inside, a tap was turned off.

'Two!'

The door handle swivelled.

'Three!'

Out sailed Estelle.

Now I'm not known for a natty dresser myself. And the person I end up looking at most often on the average day is probably Chopper, who goes round, frankly, looking like walking jumble. But still the sight of Estelle gave me a bit of a shock. She floated out wearing a shocking pink tank top full of holes through which acres of skin showed. The hem of her skirt looked as if a gang of starving ferrets had been chewing it. And on her head there was a woolly bobble hat.

Mum wellied in.

'You can't go to school in that lot!'

Smirking, Estelle trumped her.

'Fine by me!'

Quickly, Mum changed her mind.

'Yes, you can! Go off like that if you want. What do I care? What you wear to school isn't my problem, it's theirs, so let them sort it out.' She had a wild look in her eyes as she chuntered on the way Gran does about the state of next door's dustbins. 'Teachers get paid, don't they? It's their job . . . and if that Mr Scotbeg and Miss Sullivan between them don't have the sense to insist on a modest and sensible school uniform . . . only themselves to blame . . . can't expect other busy working people to—'

She broke off, distracted.

'What's that stuff on your eyes?'

'Aubergine frost.'

'Aubergine frost!'

I thought she was going to take off again about that, but she just gave a shudder, and shooed Estelle towards the stairs. I trailed behind because I thought I might get the chance to break in and ask Estelle if she had any of her allowance left that I could borrow to use for lunch money. But Mum was still ranting away as they reached the kitchen.

'Personally, I don't care any longer...done my best...if the Powers-that-Be at that school are so slack they don't mind you girls wandering up and down the corridors looking like dockside tarts...'

Dad interrupted the flow by putting his hands on Mum's shoulders and swivelling her round to face the clock.

08:47 hours.

'Oh, God!'

Mum got a grip on herself.

'Right! Got everything, Estelle? Coat? Gloves? Lunch money?'

I tried. I did try.

'Now that you mention lunch money—'

But no one was listening. Together Mum and Dad were herding Estelle towards the door. She didn't resist. But once she was out on the doorstep she turned to deliver a short speech.

'Listen, you can force me out the door. And I suppose you can even force me to school, out of the rain. But you can't force me to listen to anything the teachers say. And you can't force me to learn anything.'

Dad knows when he's on to a good thing.

'Done!' he said. 'It's a deal!'

And before she could snatch away her hand, he had shaken it to make a bargain.

She gave him one of her seek-and-exterminate looks. But he ignored it.

'Right, then,' he said cheerily. 'Off you go. Take care crossing the main road. Try not to be too late. Have a nice day.'

Then he closed the door gently behind her and leaned his forehead against it. *Thud, thud, thud, thud.* He was beating his head on the panels while Mum quietly sank at the table and buried her head in her arms.

I stared at both of them. They were *destroyed*.

After a bit, Dad pulled himself together, stopped his head-banging and said:

'Right, Bridget. You're next.'

Mum shook her buried head.

'It's no good, George. I can't go. I'm too shattered.'

'Nonsense, Bridget. Got to go to *work*.'

She lifted her head and glared at him.

'George, there's no point. I'm so exhausted I

wouldn't be able to do anything. I wouldn't even hear what my clients were saying. There's simply no sense in my going. I'll just stay home.'

But anyone who can tip Estelle out to school when she doesn't feel like going is on easy street getting Mum off to work. He simply tugged her to her feet, and stuffed her arms down her coat sleeves.

'Got everything?' he asked. 'Purse? Briefcase? Keys?'

Mum turned on him. It was an action replay of Estelle.

'Listen, George,' she snapped. 'You can force me out of the door. And you can probably force me to go to the office, out of the rain. But you can't force me to sit at my desk and do anything useful!'

As I said, Dad recognizes when he's on to a winner.

'Fine! Done!' He steered her to the door, tugging it open with one hand and shovelling her through it with the other. 'Bye, Bridget. Drive carefully now. Watch out for that nasty right turn by Budgens.'

Then, for the second time that morning, he closed the door and rested his head against the panels.

Thud, thud, thud, thud.

I was about to tackle him on the subject of dinner money, when:

Ting-a-ling-a-ling!

He sprang back as if he'd been scorched.

The door flew open, nearly hitting him. But it wasn't Mum again. It was Estelle. She stood on the doorstep – an avenging angel in a bobble hat – glowering malignantly as she reached for her book bag.

Before she left, she fixed Dad with the evil eye.

'I hope you know,' she said, 'that I only get one life. Yes. One. And it'll probably only be a few years before I'm too ancient and decrepit to enjoy it.'

'Hang on!' Dad argued. 'I'm well over forty myself and—'

She gave him a rattlesnake glare. He fell silent.

'And you are forcing me to use up my precious life!' she said. 'Spoil it. Waste my days! Why *should* I be stuck in that smelly useless classroom hour after hour, day after day, week after week, when I could be out and *alive*!'

He stood accused, while she took off down the path again, shouting over her shoulder:

'You'll be *sorry* if I get run over. If I die young,

you'll feel so rotten! You'll wish you'd let me *live*. You'll die of *guilt*.'

I was impressed. Not just because, when it comes to putting on a good curse, my sister and Miss Adulewebe come out of the same box. But also because, in what she said, there was such an echo of William Saffery. I might have been standing there listening to him in his khaki, not her in her shocking pink. He crawled, exhausted, out of a dug-out one day at dawn. The sky was awash with pink and golden fingers. The air was still. There were no birds – for months, he said, there had been nowhere for the birds to sing – but by his foot he found a baby mole, and scooped it up and felt its little heart thump, and knew in that moment, he says, the value of life, and that each dawn is a gift, and from that day he'd prize each glittering moment as if it were the most precious treasure.

Dad's voice broke into my thoughts. For just a moment it seemed he must be reading my mind, because of what he said.

'That's War for you.'

But he was only being Brigadier Flowers.

I reached down for my book bag.

'Dad, I need lunch money.'

He picked up his jacket. 'Come on,' he said.

'Let's go and look in the van. There are always coins rattling about in it somewhere. And I can give you a lift.'

He stood back to let me out. As I went by, I looked at the clock for the last time. Impeccable War Reporter getting it right.

09:07 hours.

LATE.

Chapter 5

I sometimes think Estelle leads a charmed life. I sneak in the back door and get savaged by Miss Sullivan. ('Late! Late! Can't you even keep your eye on a clock in the morning, Will Flowers?') Estelle strolls in the front, and Scotbags all but offers to carry her bag as far as the classroom for her. I overheard them in the corridor. Estelle was saying, 'A bit of a difficult time . . .' I thought at first she must be rather delicately trying to skive out of games, but when I ran into Chopper round the next corner, he said exactly the same.

'A bit of a difficult time . . .'

'What is?'

He pointed to a notice on the board, reminding all Intermediate year pupils that their parents were supposed to be in the school hall at seven thirty for a meeting.

ANNE FINE

'Daft time to pick,' he said. 'Last episode of *Who Killed Anton Dec?*'

'You're not invited,' I reminded him. 'For one thing you're no longer an Intermediate, and for another you're not yet a parent.'

Chopper's eyes gleamed.

'But it's the Great Secret Briefing.'

'Is it?' I calculated back. Yes. Though I could remember it still as if it were yesterday, it must have been a year ago to the month.

'So it is!'

Chopper grinned.

'It was tremendous,' he tempted me. 'It was *amazing.*'

It was, too. Chopper and I had been detailed to come back into school after the cleaners had gone home, to put out chairs. Chopper set up a race, and so by a few minutes after seven we had finished the job, but the school was still practically empty.

I'd looked at Chopper. Chopper had looked at me. Then, while I kept a look-out, he had pushed back the gleaming brass bolt on the door that leads under the school stage. Forbidden Territory. Danger Zone. Month after month we'd stood together, belting out hymns and eyeing that little brass bolt. We weren't going to let this opportunity slip by.

Chopper had crawled in, grumbling about filth on his trousers. I scrambled after, pulling the door closed behind me in case any of the teachers or the janitor glanced in the hall as they went past, and noticed it was open.

Chopper sneezed violently, twice. But gradually his nose adjusted to the dusty air, while I got used to the dark.

'Look at all this stuff!'

It was incredible. Leftovers from every stage production since the school was built: swords, masks, fans, cradles, cardboard rocks, a dinosaur's tail, boxes of crowns and pedlars' trays – even a mock-up of a full-size scaffold lay on its side, complete with shrouded corpse. Costumes were heaped in piles, beards strewn about, and wigs overflowed from a battered old laundry basket I hadn't forgotten spending a miserable twenty minutes squashed inside when I was one of Ali Baba's forty thieves.

'Looks like your sister's bedroom,' Chopper said.

I picked Cleopatra's plastic asp out of the Mad Hatter's teapot, and waved it in front of his face.

'Remember the way Marisa screamed?'

Slices of light through the stage boards above lit up his happy smile.

'Best detention ever!'

'We'll have another, if we don't get out.'

There is, says William Saffery, a sixth sense that stays hidden until you need it. A man's about to reach for the precious letter from home, and suddenly instead he throws himself into the mud. The shell explodes, taking two lives and twenty letters with it, and leaving him to bury more good men and wonder what is happening on the farm – and further down the line. How many brothers does he still have now? Three? One? None? I'd grabbed at Chopper's arm as he reached out to push the stage door open. Together we froze as, across the hall, came steady footfalls.

Then Chopper's eyes met mine as the one upright bar of light rolled up inside itself and disappeared.

We heard the bolt rammed home.

More and more footfalls were filling the hall now, along with the clatter of heels, the scraping of chairs and the burble of conversation.

Chopper swore under his breath. Then he despaired. Snatching the length of rope with which Stormer Phillips strangled Flora every night when she was Duchess of Malfi, he set about garrotting himself quietly. I settled on one of HMS *Pinafore*'s capstans (an upturned bucket with a nasty rim), and put my head in my hands.

First I heard nothing but parents jabbering away to one another, calling out greetings and catching up on news. Then, as the minutes passed, a sort of restlessness set in. I could see through a split between two boards. Parents in the front rows were looking at their watches, or craning round to stare at the clock on the back wall.

And then, at last, the meeting had begun. Clop-clop-clopping down the aisle from the swing doors came Mr Scotbeg and Miss Sullivan. She was in her Chief Prison Officer get-up. He wore his usual sports jacket. Together they strode towards the stage and the gossiping quietened to a murmur.

She wheeled towards the right. He followed her. And suddenly, above our heads, Chopper and I heard their footfalls reverberating across the boards of the stage.

'Good evening, everyone . . .'

There was a swell of response, and Scotbags' shoes thundered overhead, puffing down over us the clouds of fresh dust that marked his progress to the front of the stage.

'Each year,' he boomed, 'Miss Sullivan and I invite all the parents of Intermediate year pupils to this meeting. Your sons and daughters are not invited, and that is deliberate.' There was a little pause. I think he must have been leaning forward confidentially, because the next bit came out in a dramatic whisper.

'For what we have to say to you tonight is not for their ears!'

It all sounded a bit cryptic. I'd glanced at Chopper to see what he made of it, but to my astonishment he was bent over with his face buried in his knees, covering as much of his head as he could with a large floppy hat. The rope with which Stormer Phillips strangled Flora trailed to the floor, and for one awful moment I thought Chopper might have accidentally throttled himself.

Then, worse, I realized he was going to sneeze. '*Chooooo!*'

Above our heads, the secret briefing halted in mid-stream. There was a stir of interest round the hall – chairs creaking as their occupants leaned forward, and hurried little whispers down the rows. 'Did you hear something?' 'What on earth was that?'

'*Chooooo!*'

I sat on my upturned bucket and waited for death. If Chopper hadn't sneezed all over it so thoroughly, I might even have reached for the rope.

'*Chooooo! Chooooo! Chooooooo! Chooooooo!*'

How long was it before the bolt flew back? William Scott Saffery says he learned that fear can make time stretch so much it's hard to think you're still in the same world as the fast ticking clockwork and swiftly revolving steel hands that you were watching only moments before. And certainly it seemed an age before light flooded in, almost blinding us, and Chopper and I staggered out.

We stood in front of them, a hallful of mothers and fathers, all parked on the chairs that Chopper and I had set out. We must have looked a proper pair. Even then, a year ago, I was nearly as tall as I am now, but Chopper was still tiny. I bet we looked ridiculous standing side by side, blinking and sneezing, with Chopper still wearing his huge floppy hat.

Miss Sullivan leaned over the edge of the stage

to give us a long and blistering look, while Scotbags inflated his poison ducts and pointed to the door.

'Nine o'clock tomorrow morning, lads?' he suggested. 'Outside my office.'

We set off for the swing doors. I don't know what it was that made Chopper lose his senses. The awful silence? All those pairs of eyes?

Whatever it was, when we were halfway down the aisle it suddenly got to him.

'Don't worry, everyone,' he announced in ringing tones. 'It was only a *stage* we were going through.'

I don't know for certain who it was who got the joke first. I could have sworn it was Mum's laugh; but she insisted afterwards that it was Marisa's mother, and not her, who started everyone off. Within a few moments everyone in the hall seemed to be hooting with laughter. My mother had tears pouring down her face. My dad was clutching his chair. I was mortified. But Chopper took to it like someone born to please the cheering crowds.

'Thank you,' he said, sweeping the huge floppy hat off his head and turning to left and right, bowing and grinning like some triumphant actor taking his tenth curtain call. 'Thank you so much. Thank you.'

One or two of the parents took up the joke, and started to clap. Others joined in, and soon the ripple of clapping ran backwards through the hall, louder and louder, till it was steady thunderous applause, marred only by the two sets of bone-rotting gamma rays directed at us from the stage.

I took Chopper's arm.

'You do understand,' I whispered, 'that you and I are doing to *die* tomorrow?'

He didn't care. I think I've mentioned before that Chopper's not bright. All the attention was rushing to his brain, quite overwhelming the few bits that do generally keep working. He was still grinning in rapture and flourishing his hat as I pulled him through the swing doors.

Next morning was bad enough. But after we'd got out of Scotbags' room and peeled off our smouldering socks, Chopper insisted that the worst of it was still not having any idea at all what had gone on at the meeting. Personally, I was a lot more bothered by all Scotbags' ugly talk about suspension. But Chopper became obsessed. *Why* had our parents been invited without us? *What* was not for our ears?

'This year was good fun,' he kept saying. 'This year was interesting enough. But next year we'll do a really good job of sneaking in early and hiding properly. Next year we must stay long enough to hear what they say.'

The trouble with people like Chopper is that, once they get an idea into their heads, they simply won't let up. So now twelve months had gone by, both of us were a whole year older, and yet here was Chopper sticking firmly to Plan A in his bone-headed fashion.

All day I tried to tell him it wasn't worth the risk. Suppose we were caught again? We'd be expelled. But he wouldn't even bother to give the idea houseroom.

'We won't get caught. We'll hide on the balcony and watch through those holes they drilled for the wiring. We'll keep our heads below the parapet. We'll be quite safe.'

Famous Last Words. William Scott Saffery said things were so bad at Ypres no one would think of tempting fate by saying them aloud. He even tells about a night when Chalky White fell in a fearless mood and tried to get William to crawl with him across the freshly damaged stretch of trench, to reach the rest of the unit. After one last barrage, the guns fell silent, so William was willing enough. Together they inched closer to the gap, where now there was no protection. Then out of the blue, as if he were voicing a charm to protect himself, Chalky said: 'We'll be quite safe.'

Instantly, William went berserk. With all the strength at his command, he threw himself on his friend and pulled him down. When Chalky struggled to rise, William hit him, yelling: 'We can't go now! Don't you *see*? Now you've said that, we can't go!' Chalky was by far the more powerful of the two. Pushing William off, he clambered to his feet. 'Fool!' he yelled back. 'You great bl—!' There would have been a stream of it, William claims. When Chalky took to swearing, nothing could usually stop him. This time the blast from the shell wiped out the rest, and plenty more besides, as Chalky and William stood in the devil's rain, and even Chalky's 'Thanks, mate,' was drowned by the howling of the shells further along the line. Together the two of them inched through the filthy bitter wall of smoke and flying earth to drag back whichever poor fellow it was who must have been trying to cross the gap the other way, and now lay out there in the splintered dark.

But I can't throw myself on Chopper and pin

him down. If Chopper decides we're sneaking back after supper to eavesdrop a parents' meeting, then back we go. I've never understood how friendship works. Neither did William Saffery. All I know is, when Chopper, who isn't bright, said to me firmly: 'Quarter past seven. On the balcony. Right?' I, who have brains enough, only said: 'Right!'

Chopper and I chummed home. We got to his house first, but since he was still busy plotting our separate routes to the balcony, he didn't peel off. He just chummed me on to my house. Then I chummed him back. So as it happens it was after five by the time I got back again and walked into the kitchen. Mum was already home.

'Have a good day, dear?'

I was just wondering whether or not I had, when she said, 'That's good!' and went back to making up her shopping list. She's not a good listener, my mother. I'd never dream of taking her one of my problems. There'd be no point. My mother is one of those people who's busy telling you what you ought to have done even before you've had time to finish saying what you did do. And with Dad standing outside Budgens waiting for her to show up with the shopping list, she wouldn't even be trying.

I turned to Muffy, who was at the table prodding her finger in the honey on her toast, and seeing how high she could lift each strip before it fell back on her plate again. Sometimes I wonder a little about Muffy. What goes on in her brain?

'Don't mess with it,' I told her. 'Eat it.'

Mistake! Six little words, but they were quite enough to remind Mum how very capable I am.

'Will,' she said. 'Be an angel. Look after Muffy while I'm gone.'

And she was out the back door.

Explain to me, please, just how it is that every time my mother and father disappear to do the weekly shop, Estelle always seems to have disappeared even faster. I let Muffy climb onto my lap, and must have read *Rumpelstiltskin* to her at least four times before I finally heard bathwater gurgling down the pipes, and Estelle floated in and started banging through the cabinets, looking for something to eat.

'Sssh!' I warned. 'Muffy's almost asleep.'

Muffy uncorked her thumb and said, 'No, I'm not,' but Estelle couldn't have cared less in any case.

'Are we out of crunchy granola?'

'You won't have to wait long,' I told her. 'They're at the supermarket now.'

'Good.'

She plonked herself down at the table. She looked a fright. Her hair was all over the place, as if she had gone to some trouble to tangle it, and the fluffy pink dressing gown Gran gave her for Christmas was buttoned up wrong from the collar to the hem.

It's not like me to be suspicious. But, then again, it isn't like Estelle to be ready for bed by six o'clock.

'Why are you in your dressing gown?' I asked. And then, when I saw her smile: 'What are you wearing underneath?'

Still smiling, she fiddled with each button in turn, then whipped open the two halves of the dressing gown and flashed us.

Muffy's thumb fell out of her mouth. I was shocked, too. Estelle looked as if she'd stepped out of a horror film. She might have been Dracula's daughter. She was dressed all in black: black blouse, black skirt, black tights. When I say 'dressed', I'm being generous, because the blouse was slipping off her shoulders, the skirt was all fringe, and the fishnet holes in her tights were enormous. Around her neck hung loop after loop of silver chain. As for her silver belt, it was made up from so many jagged splinters that when Estelle moved and it caught the light, it was quite painful to look at.

Slipping her hand in her dressing-gown pocket, she drew out a heap more jewellery and spilled it onto the table. There it lay: dagger earrings, bracelets, scorpion rings.

Muffy looked thrilled.

'What's going on?' I asked. 'Where are you going all dressed up like that?'

Estelle gave one of her irritating smiles and tossed her head. But she wouldn't answer.

'I know,' I said. 'It's Friday night. And you still think you're going to Alison's party!'

'I don't *think*,' Estelle said loftily. 'I *am*.'

I shook my head.

'They'll never let you. It might have been all right while they still thought you meant the Alison from the swimming club. But from the moment they realized you meant Stormer Phillips's big sister, you never stood a chance.'

Estelle got up and slammed out.

I thought for a while I'd put my foot in it. Estelle has always hated hearing the truth when it doesn't fit with her plans. Those kings and queens who used to kill the messenger had nothing on Estelle, who once swiped me simply for reminding her, as she walked out of the door with her towel and her costume, that our local swimming pool was closed for repairs.

But no. Just as Muffy and I were settling into our four-millionth reading of *Rumpelstiltskin*, she suddenly appeared again, carrying her huge box of make-up and hair stuff.

I didn't see why I shouldn't say what I thought.

'No point in tarting up. You know they're not going to let you go.'

I expect there are tigers less bad-tempered than my sister.

'Listen,' she snarled. 'Mind your own business, will you? Keep your nose out of this.'

'I'm only telling you.'

She rooted in the box, spilling a whole lot of stuff that rolled off the edge of the table, where Muffy snatched at it. Estelle started doing something weird to her face with silver gunge, and Muffy pulled the top off some sort of apricot putty and started copying her. As fast as I prised one thing out of Muffy's hand, she grabbed for another. Meanwhile Estelle finished grouting and greasing. Now she could speak again.

'They'll have to let me go,' she said. 'Practically everyone in my whole year is going. We're meeting at half past nine.'

'Half past nine! Where?'

She gave me one of her cool wouldn't-you-like-to-know looks, and started in on her eyes.

'Is it at Alison's house?'

'Of course not!' Estelle scoffed. 'There wouldn't be anywhere near enough room.'

'Is it – at the Baptist Church Hall?'

Estelle's silver lip curled.

I tried again, feeling like someone in a fairy tale offered their third and last guess.

'Is it – at that club? *Fiends*?'

The old storytellers were *brilliant*. My sister was so cross that, like little Rumpelstiltskin, she stamped her foot. Muffy stopped dabbing her nose and cheeks with measles of Green Apple Eye Stick and looked a bit nervous. Estelle gave me one of her evil stares. But I didn't let her rays drain my crystals. I simply said:

'They'll never let you go. *Fiends* is famous for smoking and drinking. And worse.'

'Maybe they don't know that.'

'Maybe they do.' Suddenly a thought struck me. 'You'll have to tell them where you're going,' I said.

She upped the radiation in her look. But I held out. And, in the end, it was Estelle who cracked.

'I'll tell them!' she snapped.

'When?'

'As soon as they get back.'

Muffy looked terrified. She may not speak much, but she isn't daft. I felt her wriggle in my lap, getting ready for one of her getaways.

Just out of curiosity, I asked Estelle:

'Which one are you going to ask, Mum or Dad?'

She shrugged.

'Depends which one is here.'

'They'll both be here. They'll both be back from Budgens any minute.'

If I was smearing things that near my eyes, I wouldn't keep on talking.

'Yes, I know that. But one of them will have to go straight out again, to this parents' meeting.'

I tipped Muffy out of my lap and went across to check the calendar.

'*She* won't go out again,' I said. 'She had clients all morning, a meeting this afternoon, and it looks from this as if, in her lunch hour, she had to go to the bank, pay the road tax, and get tickets for that puppet show for Muffy. By the time she gets back from shopping, all she'll want is a long bath.'

Estelle looked up, startling me with spook's eyes.

'Well, *he* won't be going,' she said. 'He told me his mechanic is off sick, and he was going to have to man the telephones and do the servicings, as well as keeping his eye on that new girl on the forecourt. And he's gone shopping too. So all he'll want when he gets back is to fall onto the sofa and watch *Who Killed Anton Dec?* on telly.'

'Maybe they'll skip it . . .'

Estelle laughed. And she was right. The day those two skip a school meeting will be the day they pack Muffy off to college on a train.

'No,' I agreed, leaning against the door. 'One of them will go.'

There was the sound of footsteps outside. Estelle drew her fluffy pink dressing gown more tightly around her, and I was thrown halfway across the room by the sheer force of the door flying open. Mum staggered in, behind a huge box of groceries.

'*You* go, George,' she was saying. 'I'm not going. I had the most awful clients all morning, a

ANNE FINE

frightful meeting that lasted almost all afternoon, and I had to use up my lunch hour going to the bank, paying the road tax, and getting tickets for that puppet show for Muffy. Not to mention going shopping. All I want is a long, hot bath.'

Dad followed her in, carrying two more boxes, one on top of the other.

'Well, *I'm* not going,' he said. 'You know my mechanic's off sick. All day I've had to look after the telephones as well as taking care of the servicings, and keeping an eye on young Sarah. And I've been shopping too. The only thing I want to do is to put my feet up and watch telly.'

'Maybe just this once we could skip it . . .'

Dad dumped his shopping down and gave her a look.

'No,' Mum agreed. 'I suppose one of us will have to go.'

She stopped pulling tins of soup out of the box and had a look around. It was unfortunate that the first thing she saw was Muffy's face.

'My God!'

'It's all right,' I said. 'There's nothing wrong with her. She's just been mucking about with Estelle's make-up.'

So then Mum looked at Estelle.

110

'My God!'

'It's all right,' I said. 'There's nothing wrong with her either. It's just she's going out.'

Dad came across to take a closer look. Then he said, 'Not looking like that, she isn't,' and wandered off to unpack the washing powder without even noticing Estelle was delivering him one of her microwave attacks, and marking him down in her Hate Book.

You could see Mum decide to approach things a shade more tactfully.

'Where are you going, dear?' she asked Estelle – quite nicely, I thought, considering that Mum had been fighting her way around Budgens and Estelle had been lounging in a bath. 'Are you nipping down the library before it closes?'

Good job that at that moment she'd turned her back to shovel soups on a shelf. She didn't see the look on Estelle's face.

But she did notice there was no reply, because she tried again. 'Or are you going to help Mrs Hurley with the Brownies?'

I don't know about Mum, but I could feel the temperature in the room dropping to zero. I'm like William Scott Saffery. The one thing I can't stand is those few moments of icy calm before an attack. Once William 'accidentally' fired his rifle simply to end the grim wait. I'm exactly the same.

The words just popped out.

'She says she's going to *Fiends*.'

Did I say the room was pretty cold before? Now we were down to glacial permafrost.

'Oh, I don't think so, dear. It's getting a bit late.'

'Late! It's not even half past six! It's still daylight!'

Mum eyed the kitchen window suspiciously, as if unconvinced that all that bright stuff outside was proper daylight. Then she changed tack.

'Tonight's not a good night, dear.'

'Tonight's when it's *on*!'

Mum ignored this.

'And anyway,' she persisted. 'It's silly to get dressed all over again, now you're in your dressing gown and slippers.'

What gave the game away? Estelle didn't speak or move. I think Mum must read minds. Because, passing the bargain pack of scouring pads in her hand over to Dad, she stepped across the room and – slowly, carefully – unbuttoned Estelle's pink dressing gown.

Muffy hid her head in her hands. My stomach

knotted. Dad looked quite shattered when he saw the skirt.

And Mum went mad.

'Listen to me, young lady. You can go straight upstairs and take off those horrible clothes. If you think for one moment that your father and I are going to let you walk out of this house looking like *that*—'

Words failing Mum for a moment, Estelle took her chance.

'Look, Mum!' she said. 'I'm not Muffy. I'm me! I'm not in nursery school. I'm an Intermediate. And I'm old enough to go out with my friends.'

'You're not old enough to go to *Fiends*.'

'Why not?'

'Because we've heard all about that club, that's why,' Dad broke in sharply. 'And seen the types hanging around outside, smoking and swigging from their bottles. And *worse*.'

Estelle stuck her hands on her hips. (Firing position 1.) Muffy scrambled into my lap and, opening *Rumpelstiltskin*, put on a blank face and pretended she wasn't listening. She looked so unconcerned you'd never have guessed she was bothered in the slightest unless you knew, as I do, that Muffy can't stand missing a single word in any of her favourite stories. And she was staring down at page fifteen.

Estelle was definitely out of her basket now.

'I'm *not* too young. I'm not! You just don't understand how things are these days. *Everyone* in my year is allowed to smoke. *Everyone*'s allowed to drink. And *everyone*'s allowed to go out to *Fiends*. I've made arrangements. You can't treat me like a baby. You have to let me go! You can't keep me locked in this box!'

Mistake! Mistake!

'Box?' You'd think from the dangerously calm tone of Mum's voice that Estelle's life expectancy was now measurable in seconds. 'What box is this, Estelle? I'm looking round for a box.'

Sarcastically, she made the gesture of glancing to left and right. Then, like a flare shooting up to light the sky:

'This isn't a *box*, Estelle! This is a *home*! A home your father and I have slaved for years to—'

Muffy was tugging desperately at my woolly, trying to pull it down safely over her head. But suddenly Mum stopped. She just broke off. It was extraordinary, as if the flare, instead of sailing in its customary brilliant arc across the sky, had settled directly into a sizzling downward trail before spluttering out into blackness.

'Oh, *you* tell her, George! I can't be bothered.'

Mum reached for her shoulder bag and undid the flap, checking she had her keys. 'I'll slip away to the parents' meeting, and you stay here and explain to Estelle why she can't go out tonight.'

I've never seen Dad move so fast in my life. If Mum had been a live football, and the back door the goal, he couldn't have moved more smartly to make the save.

'Oh, no! Oh, no, no, no. *I'll* go to the parents' meeting. You stay here.'

'No, *really*, George,' said Mum. (She sounded so sweet and reasonable that Muffy even lifted up the edge of my woolly to peep in amazement.) 'Your mechanic was off sick, and you had to answer the telephones and do the servicings, as well as keeping your eye on Sarah. And you've been out shopping too. What you ought to do is settle down on the sofa, put your feet up and watch telly.'

It must be Courtesy Week at 27 Beechcroft Avenue.

'No, no,' said Dad. 'Don't be ridiculous, Bridget. You had horrible clients all morning and then a meeting that went on practically all afternoon, and you didn't even get a proper lunch hour because you had to go to the bank, pay the road tax and get tickets for that puppet show for Muffy. And you came shopping too. So what you need now is a nice long hot bath.'

'No, no,' Mum said. 'I'll go. You stay.'

'No, no,' insisted Dad. 'You stay. I'll go.'

They were so taken up with making their chivalrous offers, they didn't sense the rocket going off.

'Fine!' Estelle exploded. 'Oh, lovely! Really nice for me! First you gang up to stop me having any fun! And then you fight to see who can get out of giving me one good reason why I should lead this boring, miserable life! You're both mean and selfish and horrible!'

This time Muffy pulled the front of my woolly so far down over her head, her mop of hair came spilling out of my neck hole.

Dad took a very deep breath.

'Now listen to me, Estelle—'

'No!' she howled. 'No, I won't! Ever since I could talk you've been telling me to listen! I'm not listening any longer! I've had enough!'

She wrenched the door to the hall open so

hard that, under the cover of my woolly, Muffy still heard it and reached up to put her hands over her ears.

Bang!!!

The whole house shook.

Dad sighed.

'I don't know,' he said. 'Sometimes I wonder how this house stays upright, the way Estelle slams doors.'

He swung round.

'Bridg—' He stopped, aghast. 'Bridget? Bridget, where are you? Bridget!'

Muffy peeped through the stretched neck hole of my woolly like some little baby kangaroo peeping from its mother's pouch.

'What happened?' Dad demanded.

'Nothing happened,' I told him. 'Mum just picked up her bag and left.'

'I didn't hear her go.'

I shrugged. If Dad hasn't learned by now Estelle can slam doors plenty loud enough for two, he can't have been paying attention.

'When will she be back?'

'The meeting will be over by nine.'

'Nine!'

He glanced at the ceiling. There was a look of

terror on his face. It was a bit like a moment in a horror film where everyone trapped in the room sees the plaster bulging overhead from the gathering evil forces.

'I suppose I'd better go up there and sort her out.' He didn't move. He seemed to need to convince himself first. 'She did seem a little upset.'

Then Muffy spoke.

'Poor Stelly . . .'

William Scott Saffery said he never knew how each man got himself over the top, knowing what lay beyond. In some, it looked like blind courage. Others, he suspected, still half-believed in what they were doing. For quite a few, it was the fear of being thought a coward, whether you were one or not. Some had their officers' guns stuck in their backs, of course. But William thought the great majority ended up clambering over to their deaths simply because there were other men watching.

We watched him watch us watching him. Then Good Old Brigadier Flowers pulled himself up and straightened his shirt in his trousers.

'Right, then,' he said. 'I'm going up.'

Muffy slid off my knee and padded across to him. He lifted her up, not even bothering to try and persuade her to stay downstairs with me, and listen to *Rumpelstiltskin*. There was no point. Muffy adores Estelle so much she'd rather know exactly what's going on than sit imagining it. I understand that. And William Saffery says sometimes he thought that was the only reason he himself ended up putting his foot up on the ledge of mud he knew might be the last bit of the world he'd ever see, once signals ran down the line.

With Muffy in his arms, Dad walked towards the door.

I followed, and watched him climbing heavily up the stairs, with Muffy on his back. She might have been a rucksack, the way she kept her arms clamped round his neck, and her legs tightly drawn up.

Upstairs, doors banged ferociously, and the house shook. But Dad pressed on, tread by tread.

Over the top.

Chapter 6

Y ou can't be blamed for your good spirits, once you've got out of danger. As Corporal MacFie said so many times that William itched to wring his neck: 'Sorry it's him. But glad it wasnae me.'

I hared down the path, jumped the Muffy-proof gate, and shot off up the road, leaping at every overhanging tree to strip off a few leaves. I didn't realize I was chewing them till I fetched up on a laurel. But by then I was too near school to spit them out without checking first that no one who gets to write in Wallace School's Book of Sinners had got me in their sights.

I looked around.

There seemed to be an awful lot of faces I recognized, staring at me through car windows. Parents making their way to the meeting! I speeded up again, and nearly got run over several times, sprinting along the lane that leads to the car park. The tyre factory clock said ten past seven. I was late. But jumping for another leaf without thinking, I noticed Chopper snaking his way along the high wall behind Budgens. I did my Randy Cat, and he yowled back. But I carried on the long way. Personally, I'd rather get run down than fall off a wall into brambles. Everyone likes to do things in their own way. Obviously the parents weaving past in their cars prefer to get to meetings dead on time. My mum and dad leave home at the last minute and end up sitting somewhere in the four back rows, grumbling that they can't hear.

But not tonight. In her great hurry to get out of the house, Mum must have been one of the first. Certainly she'd managed to get one of the parking spaces near the gate, all set for her next speedy getaway. I made a point of sticking close to the wall, in case she was still about. But all I saw were other people's parents slamming their car doors and locking up, and striding to the main entrance.

I slid in the back way and made it down the stairs and along two corridors, leaping from the cover of one doorway to the next, before I heard footsteps and voices. I darted into the cloakroom, and when the voices seemed to come nearer, crouched on a bench and wrapped myself inside Marisa's bright yellow cape. It reeked of perfume. You can take it from me – in a tight space, *Soir de Paris* is worse than the smell Mr Astley complains about when people skip showers, and Miss Adulewebe used to refer to loftily as '*Essence d'aisselle*'.

The voices came closer and closer. I realized suddenly that I knew one of them.

'This isn't the right way at all!' No doubt about it. No one complains like Mum. 'You might teach orienteering and survival skills, but you've brought us down the wrong corridor. Surely the hall is on the other side.'

Orienteering? Survival skills? Then I must know the other voice as well.

'Sorry. All my fault. Losing my grip.'

I nearly fell off the bench. Chopper's dad! He didn't have a child in Intermediates, like Mum, so what was he doing hanging around the school at this time in the evening? Not kicking off another of his fiendish 'Start Orienteering' courses, surely. It had been months ago, but I still hadn't forgotten some of the bad times. Twice a week for a whole term, he'd fastened his fangs in the back of my legs for holding my map upside down when, to my mind, I'd already proved I wasn't of sound mind by signing up for the course in the first place. Now the huge beefy bruiser was warbling soft apologies. It was a good thing Chopper wasn't here, listening to my mum running his old man through her portable self-esteem shredder.

'I thought you were a professional army man, Mr Chopperly! Surely they must have taught you how to find your way through deserts and swamps, and dropped you into jungles with no food and no maps. How could someone with your expertise get lost following a few cardboard "This Way" signs down a straight corridor?'

You'd think a trained man could take it. But suddenly the bench on which I was crouching started to shake. Clearly he'd had to sit down. When the shuddering eased off, I stirred the folds in Marisa's cape till I could see a little. He was slumped at the other end of the bench, head in his hands, the picture of despair.

'Oh, dear,' Mum was saying hastily. 'Please don't take on so. I didn't mean what I said, honestly.'

His shoulders shook.

Mum patted him on the back.

'Mr Chopperly?'

The bench trembled again. I took the opportunity to slide my back down the wall and make myself a bit more comfortable. I had the feeling that I'd be nesting in Marisa's cape a little longer than expected.

'Sorry . . .' I heard him croak. 'I'll pull myself together in a tick. I'll get a grip.'

Mum parked herself at his side.

'What's the matter? Why are you so upset? You can tell me.'

He shook his head.

'Stupid . . .' he muttered. 'I have to get a hold on myself. I have to get on top of this.'

'On top of *what*?'

He raised his head. I was a little shocked, I can tell you. Admittedly the last time I saw Chopper's dad he was dressed in his heavy-duty gear and herding me and the other victims out of the minibus after our ghastly weekend on Helvellyn. He looked hardboiled enough then. Now he looked pitiful, a shadow of himself, a trembling wreck.

Mum clearly thought so too.

'You look quite awful, Mr Chopperly. Are you ill?'

Give him his due, he's no self-pitying wimp.

'No, no. Never fitter. All systems go, truly.'

But Mum knows a broken man when she sees one.

'Trouble at home? How is your wife? Is she well?'

'Fine. Super. Tickety-boo.'

Mum ran through a quick check-list of family trouble spots.

'How about the baby? Is she sleeping?'

'Out like a light at ten. Not a peep until six. We think they must have sent an angel by mistake.'

'The twins?'

'Blooming. Splendid. Happy as sandboys, both of them. And doing very well indeed at school.'

Mistake! I expect, in the really crack regiments, they do a better job of teaching them not to get cornered so easily under skilled interrogation. The bench began to shake even before Mum slid her last little question home as quickly and cleanly as a knife between ribs.

'And how is Chopper?'

A look of terror passed across his face, as if she'd asked him: 'How's Beelzebub?'

'Chopper?'

She'd hit the spot.

'Yes, Chopper. How is he?'

The man did try. If ever the whisper runs around our school that Mr Chopperly's chicken, I'll tell them all this much: he had a go. His voice cracked, and he sounded like a liar. But he did try.

'Chopper? No trouble! None at all!'

If it hadn't been for the look of sheer incredulity on my mum's face, I think I might almost have believed him. Of course, I do know Chopper has his little troubles at home. In fact, practically every lunch hour I have to sit and listen to him going on and on about the giant great row he's just had because he left the tiniest speck of oil on his carpet, or stayed out a minute too late. Poor Chopper's problem is that, when his dad's away, his mum can't sleep until her precious son is safely tucked in bed. Since she works at the airport, starting at six, Chopper ends up arguing the toss for every last half hour out.

My mother doesn't know that. I've never really thought it all that wise to pass the message on. But still she didn't look as if she believed that life with Chopper was nothing but sunshine and roses.

'What? No trouble at all?'

The first hairline cracks appeared.

'Well, naturally, now and again we have a little spot of bother . . .'

'Spot of bother?'

Ex-army officer Chopperly raised his head and told my mother firmly:

'Boys will be boys. It's only natural.'

Mum can decode messages without the cipher.

'That bad? What on earth happened?'

His face took on a hunted look. His eyes roamed up and down the rows of pegs. If I'd not known he was in another world, trapped in his nightmare, I might have felt unsafe wrapped in the cape, hearing him spill out his story.

'It's nothing important. Nothing at all. It's just that when I came home last night I found Chopper stripping down his brand-new bike, the one we bought for his birthday.'

He tried to rally.

'Yes,' he said proudly. 'He's pretty handy with the tools!'

But Mum's no slouch when it comes to homing in on the soft parts of a story.

'A brand-new bike? Stripping it down?'

The look of pride drained away. He shook his head, and stared with haunted eyes.

'Yes! Stripping it down. It was a brand-new bike! Still shiny from the shop! And he was stripping it down!'

The next words came out so soft and strangled I could barely hear them.

'On...his...brand...new...carpet.'

Mum gasped. I didn't, since I'd heard Chopper's side of this sad tale more than once over lunchtime. I watched Mr Chopperly swing round to face Mum, his eyes flashing.

'Who *asked* for carpet in his bedroom? He did! He said it would make the room warmer. He *wanted* it.' He scrambled to his feet, and his voice rose. 'And who *paid* for it? Not him! It was his mother who worked overtime for two whole months to pay for that carpet. Two whole months!'

Now he was striding up and down between the rows of pegs.

'Guess how long it took to lay! Guess! I did it properly, you know. None of your shoddy DIY for me. I did a proper job. It took the whole weekend!'

He wheeled round like somebody on a parade ground.

'I'm a good army man. Twelve years I was with

my regiment. Twelve whole years! I'm an experienced soldier. I've seen active service three times. Three! They don't send softies into combat, you know. War is no picnic!'

He stared into nothing and nowhere, remembering . . .

'I've seen some ugly messes in my time. God knows, I've seen some messes—' His voice broke. 'But that carpet! You can't *imagine* what it looked like!'

Now *I* was gasping. I was astonished at the fuss he was making. Chopper had made a point of saying to me several times: 'That oil was a *speck*. You could hardly see it. You practically needed a microscope to know it was there!' And here was Chopper's dad, the haunted look back in force, letting my mother pat him and whisper soothing things in his ear, while he rambled on like a madman: '*Pools* of oil,' he was muttering. 'Trodden in . . . splashed up the *walls*! Great big black footprints all over . . . ruined!' And then the cry I'd heard so often before, in our own house: 'It's the senseless destruction of it! That's what I can't stand! The senseless, senseless destruction!'

Really, they do exaggerate, these parents. I felt quite irritated on Chopper's behalf. I was even considering rising from Marisa's cape like Venus from the waves to defend my good friend, when Mum started patting the bench beside her.

'Sit down,' she told Mr Chopperly. 'Sit down. I want to tell you something. Listen to this. Last week, Estelle dyed her hair in the spare room. Guess how many things she ruined. Guess!' Like someone distracting a small child, she made Chopper's dad sit down beside her again before she'd start ticking them off on her fingers. 'I'll tell you. Two snow-white bedspreads, a huge patch of wallpaper, one little furry rug, her sweater, two library books, two towels and a flannel.'

Now I know for a fact this was unreasonable. The library books were perfectly readable if you didn't worry too much about some of the descriptions. And I'd use that flannel again. (Well, I'll have to. It's mine.)

Once again, I was about to leap up and argue, but I didn't get the chance. For Mr Chopperly was off again.

'That's nothing!' he scoffed. 'Four girls came round for Chopper last Saturday. I went out for half an hour. Half an hour! When I got back, one radiator was away from the wall, the phone was cracked, and though Sadie and I have searched the house twice, we still haven't found the extension lead for the radio.'

Mum threw her head back and hooted.

'That's nothing! The day before yesterday I went into Estelle's room, and there I saw...'

I was beginning to panic. It was all right for these two, sitting here, exchanging Great Exaggerated Tales of War. I had a date with Chopper. If I could manage to lift the cape off its hook, it might be possible to keep it round me like a bilious tent, and shift my bum silently along the bench to the next peg, and on and on, till I reached the door to the showers. Time was getting on.

I concentrated on the crucial unhooking of the cape, and more snatches of conversation floated my way. I was no longer listening, but I couldn't help hearing.

'*Sick* of not being able to hear a word he says. "Speak up!" I say a million times a day. "Don't mumble at me! If you have something to say, open your mouth and say it properly"...'

'Would simply never occur to her to *ask* if she could borrow it...'

I managed to lift the loop off the peg. Cautiously, silently, I inched along the bench as more offensive snippets drifted over.

'Absolutely no consideration. "Can you pick me up at nine?" Say yes, and it's, "Well, if you're picking me up, can you take Flora home too?" And if you agree, it's, "Can we just drop Flora's cello off at her dad's place?" And after that...'

'Never knocks... Simply *barges* in...'

Was she complaining about *me*? Cheek! Still, it wasn't the moment to get up and argue. Already I was halfway along the bench. Frankly, the two of them were so immersed in their Great Grumble Session, I don't think they would have noticed if all the abandoned coats in the cloakroom had suddenly drawn themselves up on their pegs, and started making for the exits.

'...always *wanting* things. Don't seem to realize people can't have everything. For one thing, where on earth would they *put* it?'

'One minute they're acting their age. The next, you'd think that they were only *three*!'

Nearly there...

'Have to tell them everything time and again. Do you find that? You wouldn't think that they have any *brains*. You only have to tell me something once, and I remember it.'

'Never thought I'd end up pinning notices on my own walls! Can you imagine? Yesterday I found myself taping a notice to the banisters. "*No one is to muck about in the living room or in the hall or on the stairs.*" I'd even put an asterisk against the words "muck about" and added underneath: "*Mucking about is defined as any activity that is not being in simple transit between one room and another.*" Can you believe it? Notices in my own house! I thought I'd left that sort of thing behind in the barracks!'

I was about to fling off the cape and make a run for it, when I heard Mum say:

'Oh, God! Look at the time!'

They scrambled to their feet. Mr Chopperly, you could tell, was almost himself again. Without even thinking about it, Mum seemed to have sorted him out. I was pretty impressed when I thought about it. Clever old Mum. Knows nothing about the army, never touched a gun, and no experience at all of seeing men crack up under fire. And yet she'd managed to get Chopper's dad back into fighting trim in almost no time at all. He was practically bounding ahead of her now, down the long echoing corridor. Even his sense of direction seemed to be back in force. She hurried along in his wake, and I followed after, till we reached the main entrance, where I peeled off silently.

The clock on the wall informed me I was going to be as late for my date with Chopper as most of his girlfriends are. And I've heard him sounding off loudly and often enough about that over his marmalade sandwiches.

As quickly as I could, I spun up the stairs to the balcony.

Chapter 7

I'd thrown away a good few golden stars in Chopper's Book of Friends, that was for sure. The look he gave me when I finally pushed open the door was little short of Estellish.

'Where have you been?'

I padded over on all fours, keeping my head below the parapet.

'I got trapped.'

'Oh, yes? Who by?'

'My mother and your dad.'

'Blimey!'

That put an end to his pouting. He dug in his pocket and fetched out a peppermint as a peace offering. It was coated in fluff, but I took it anyway to show there was no ill-feeling.

'What's going on down there?' I whispered, nodding over the balcony. 'What have I missed?'

Chopper shrugged. He looked mystified.

'I can't work it out at all,' he complained. 'I've been plugged in since it began, honestly. I've listened to every word. But so far as I can make out, Scotbags is explaining to the parents where babies come from.'

'Come off it!' I chortled.

He simply shrugged again.

'Move over,' I ordered.

Obediently, Chopper shunted along to make room. I was about to shove my eye to a hole drilled through the parapet to take some long-abandoned wire, when Chopper took to sniffing the air.

'What's that peculiar smell?'

'Peppermint?'

He shook his head. 'No. It's sort of sickly and disgusting, with mouldy flowers on top.'

'Oh, that! That's Marisa's scent.'

Chopper looked horrified.

'You've kissed *Marisa*?'

I turned and glowered at him. He took a full dose of gamma rays before muttering an apology. Only then did I turn my attention back to the eye hole. I peered and listened for a little while. Chopper appeared to be right. Scotbags was standing at the front of the stage, waving his arms around like a windmill in a high gale, and giving the parents what appeared to be a sex talk. I tried to pay full attention, though we get revision classes on this topic so often now, I've practically trained myself to unplug at the very first mention of glands and hormones and instinctual drives. But I did listen to him boring away as long as I could stand it. Then I gave up.

Chopper was leaning back against the parapet, blowing smoke rings from an imaginary cigar.

'Has he been going on like this ever since he kicked off?' I whispered.

Chopper nodded, and picked an imaginary flake of fine tobacco from his lower lip before whispering back.

'Pedalling on about hormones since he began. I think he must have gone well beyond his allotted half-hour. You take a peek at Miss Sullivan. She looked ready to pass him The Poisoned Cocoa ten minutes ago.'

I checked it out. Chopper was right again. Miss Sullivan sat bolt upright in her prison governor blue, looking as if she had heard more than enough of all this tosh about young people and their inner storms. Even as I watched, she shifted impatiently on her chair, scraping its legs deliberately across the floorboards.

And Scotbags took the hint.

'But that's enough about the problem!' he cried. 'More to the point, what is the solution?' And off he went again, this time quoting huge chunks, word for word, out of the school prospectus. I only recognized it because, once, Miss Sullivan caught me pulling the pins out of Hope Johnson's hair, and made me learn a page and a half by heart as a punishment:

'*School is a natural forum for the development of friendships, but it often causes real embarrassment and awkwardness that boys, while fairly matched intellectually with girls, mature emotionally at such a grossly different rate . . .*'

By now Miss Sullivan was looking as if raw meat alone would satisfy her. She rattled her chair legs on the floor. She drummed her fingers on her prison skirt. She glowered horribly. It was quite clear that if Scotbags didn't hand the audience over soon, something inside her would snap.

'*It's not a question of being strict and old-fashioned for the sake of it,*' Mr Scotbeg was saying. '*Rather, we attempt to apply the rules of common sense while we regulate the social life of the boys and girls in our care.'*

He stopped. He'd come to the end of all he could remember. So, switching his affable head-master act back up to Regulo 8, he turned with a smile to Miss Sullivan.

'And I *think*,' he offered tentatively. 'I *think* it's just *possible* Miss Sullivan *might* like to add a brief word or two...'

'Fancy that!' Chopper murmured beside me.

Miss Sullivan rose to her feet and pounded towards the front of the stage with a wild gleam in her eye.

'I think this is going to be the good bit,' I told Chopper.

He blew out a leisurely smoke ring and smiled seraphically. Miss Sullivan's voice blasted over the parapet like a well-aimed grenade.

'*Parents!*' she cried.

There was a startled rattle of chair legs as even those Scotbags had bored into discreetly snoring little heaps shot back to wakefulness.

'Parents! These are dangerous times! Dangerous times!'

One or two of the parents I could see in the front rows turned their heads to glance at one another. Was the woman unhinged? Miss Sullivan paused for breath, then started off again, not like Scotbags, in the measured tones of a talking school brochure, but prowling up and down along the front of the stage, rolling her eyes like someone desperate to escape from their locked ward and warn the world about the little green men.

'Have you noticed anything strange about your children recently?'

More heads turned to one another uneasily, but she didn't notice. She batted on.

'That son of yours who used to be so pleasant and helpful and straightforward. Has he turned secretive and peculiar? Has he taken to lurking in his bedroom for hours and hours on end?'

A ripple of shock ran through the hall. It was extraordinary. Usually, even from a glance you can tell half of them are sitting there wondering if they've left the iron on, and the other half are thinking about what they're missing on telly. But suddenly scores of them were sitting bolt upright with their ears pinned back, listening as hard as they could. Miss Sullivan had only uttered a few words, and yet, even through a tiny peep-hole, you could tell that most of those sitting in front of her were totally plugged in to what she was saying.

'Has your boy become clumsy and awkward?

Has he begun to slip away to his room the moment you haul the vacuum cleaner out of the cupboard, or mention the washing-up? Does he burst through doorways like Neanderthal man?'

She dropped her voice before letting rip with the next batch of rude observations.

'Or maybe without any warning at all he's turned irritable and insolent, and started to argue all the time. And what is he *doing* up there all alone in his bedroom? You don't know, do you? But sometimes you come back from shopping or a hard day's work, and you find he's been doing something totally insane, like gluing his wood models on top of his bedspread, or stripping down his bike on a perfectly good carpet.'

I felt a sharp push. Chopper had laid aside his imaginary cigar, and was trying to force me away from the peep-hole. I thought of resisting, but it was his turn. So obediently I moved over.

'Look!' Chopper muttered bitterly. 'Look at my dad! Mouth hanging open, nodding away like an idiot! He obviously thinks she's talking directly to him!'

It seemed the right moment to ask him. 'What's your dad doing down there anyway? You're not an Intermediate.'

But Chopper slumped back on the floor in disgust, and wouldn't answer. To cheer him up, I handed him back his imaginary cigar, and stuck my eye to the hole again. Now Miss Sullivan was standing so close to the edge of the stage, you'd think she might topple over into the audience. The wild light was still in her eyes. She was pointing a finger.

'And all the rest of you!' she cried. 'What about your little girls? Changed, are they? Acting oddly? Maybe they've gone sullen and cheeky, and answer you back all the time. Maybe they've grown selfish and rude and inconsiderate, locking themselves in the bathroom for hours on end, and leaving their bits and pieces all over the place, for other people to pick up.'

Chopper gave me a nudge.

'I think she's talking about your sister now.'

Mum clearly thought so too. I had located her at last. She'd found an empty seat halfway down one of the aisles, and she was perched on the edge, rapt, like someone listening for the last number on their Bingo card. All round her, heads were nodding furiously. Miss Sullivan had obviously done her homework on girls.

'Has she become practically impossible to live

with recently?' she was demanding. 'Does she dress up in jumble and expect you to let her go out and be seen by the neighbours? If you speak to her nicely, does she snarl? In fact, if you give her a word of sensible advice about anything, does she snap your head off?'

'She is, then,' Chopper insisted. 'She's definitely talking about your sister.'

Miss Sullivan gave a little laugh. It wasn't pleasant. No, it wasn't pleasant.

'Apart from that,' she said, 'she probably hardly ever speaks. She probably hardly ever smiles.' Hastily, she corrected herself: 'Well, that's to *you*, of course. I'm sure she's still all smiles and merry chatter with her friends.'

Miss Sullivan added, 'In fact, she's probably so chatty with her friends that your last phone bill came as a bit of a shock...'

Even over the parapet we could hear the gasps of astonishment. Chopper nudged me again, nodding, and I remembered he was at our house the morning Dad ripped open one of the yellow envelopes from the phone company and took a major fit with poor Estelle.

And he wasn't the only one nodding, either. Down in the hall, the rows of heads were going up and down, up and down.

Chopper shoved me aside.

'Look at them all!' he hissed angrily. 'Loving every minute of it!'

What was the matter with him? I didn't get it at all. I mean, Chopper might have to wrangle a bit with his mother every now and again about his social life versus her beauty sleep, but that is *nothing*. If Chopper wants to know about real arguing, he ought to move to 27 Beechcroft Avenue and see Mum and the Banshee scrapping with one another like fiends out of hell. What happens in Chopper's house is probably what my dad has in mind when he suggests 'a friendly discussion'.

Personally, I don't think Chopper knows he's born.

I picked up his imaginary cigar, and blew a perfect smoke ring over his head.

'Don't get so worked up,' I whispered. 'You needn't take it personally. She isn't talking about people like you. These are parents of the Intermediates, not our year.'

Chopper turned from the peep-hole and gave me a very odd look indeed.

'We're back here tonight,' he pointed out,

'because last year we didn't stay hidden long enough to hear the talk. But it's exactly the same talk. That's why my dad's shown up. He missed it last year.'

Good thing it wasn't a real cigar. I'd have choked. Not just because it always rattles me when Chopper, who, as I may have hinted, isn't bright, works something out before I do. What threw me most was suddenly realizing that Mum and Dad must have gone through the whole of the last year with me in their sights and this speech ringing in their ears.

How would you feel about that? A bit cheesy, I'll bet.

And I don't mind just this once taking a leaf out of Miss Adulewebe's Guide Book for Unfeeling Writers and telling you I was a bit put out to think that every time I spent a bit of time upstairs scribbling away quietly in this book by myself, my mum and dad had got me marked down as being a secretive and peculiar bedroom lurker, as advertised well in advance by the Celebrated Neuro-Physiologist Mr Scotbeg, and his colleague Miss Sullivan, World-Famous Expert on Outlandish Teenage Behaviour.

'Cheek!'

Chopper pitched in, like a good mate.

'What does she know about it, anyway? Interfering old trout!'

He was making for the peep-hole again, but I shouldered him aside. It was my turn, after all. And I wanted to have another look at my mother.

Now I came to think about it, what was *she* doing here for the second time in a row? It wasn't as if she could have made a mistake about the evening's programme. By the time she and Chopper's dad finally showed up in the doorway, Scotbags had been well away unfolding his thoughts about hormones. Mum must have realized this wasn't going to be the usual order of events (Miss Sullivan thrashing about with her pointer explaining this month's changes in the national curriculum, followed by Scotbags trumpeting on in a threatening fashion about the litter piling in unsightly mounds up against the school fence, and the need for more volunteers on the fund-raising committee).

So why had my mother stayed? She's always going on about how busy she is, and how her briefcase is bulging at the seams. As soon as she realized she'd shown up for the second year in a row for exactly the same talk about steaming glands, why didn't she turn straight round and drive back home? I've caught her skulking away in the garage often enough, trying to get through tomorrow's paperwork before setting foot in the house.

Why wasn't she doing that now? Why was she still here?

Deeply curious, I singled her out again from the nodding throng. She was still perched on the edge of her seat, gazing towards the stage. Somehow the set of her head reminded me strongly of someone. For a moment I couldn't think who, but then it came to me, and I was horrified. My mum looked just like that woman in the red knitted beret who comes every Saturday to listen to the Welshman preaching in the arcade. I watched her leaning forward, mesmerized, and thought I understood at last. My mother, who hasn't been in a church as long as I can remember, had come to Hear the Word.

Which had turned into a Warning. For now Miss Sullivan drew herself up straight as a pole and repeated in spine-freezing tones:

'Dangerous times! I warn you, you must be very much *on your guard*! Any day now, that child of yours may sidle up to you—'

She minced a few steps across the stage, until she was standing by the lectern on which Scotbags rests his elbows when he's haranguing us about the way we let our bag buckles scrape the paint-work in the corridors, or drop our chocolate wrappers anywhere we please. She turned to face her audience and put on a young whiny voice.

'"Mu–um. Da–ad. Why *can't* I stay out till twelve? It isn't late."'

A few parents chuckled. She waited till they were quiet. This wasn't funny.

'Twelve o'clock *is* late,' she thundered. 'It is late, late, *late*!' She fixed them with the rattlesnake look. 'Never give in!' she commanded them. 'Don't even dream of weakening simply because you're tired of arguing today. For you will only be exhausted tomorrow, and you will have all the extra ground to make up.'

She stopped, to let her reasoning sink in. They were all paying the greatest attention. There was absolute silence. Even Scotbags looked transfixed.

When she spoke again, it was in a low voice. The conspiratorial whisper ran through the hall and up, up, over the parapet, like a chill wind.

'For your children are cunning,' she warned. 'Very, very cunning. They will try to get around you. Listen to some of the things they will say.'

She tipped her head and cupped a hand to her ear, as if to listen to her own wheedling imitation.

'"Mu–um. Da–ad. You don't know how things are in our school. *Everyone*'s allowed to smoke . . ."'

Her hand came crashing down on the lectern.

'*No one*'s allowed to smoke!'

Again she tipped her head and cupped her hand to hear herself wheedling: '"*Everyone*'s allowed to drink . . ."'

The hand crashed down.

'*No one*'s allowed to drink!'

She cupped her hand for the third time, as if to catch the faraway bleat of some forlorn lost lamb.

'"But Mu–um. Da–ad. *Everyone*'s allowed to go to bars and clubs . . ."'

The hand came down so hard I thought the lectern might split. Her face was purple.

'*No one*'s allowed to go to bars or nightclubs! United we stand and divided we fall. You must *all stick together*!'

An electric charge ran through the hall. You'd think that every one of them had been poked with a cattle prod, the way they shot up in their seats. The women sat taller. Some of the men's elbows jutted out at their sides, and I couldn't think why, till I realized that they were straightening their ties. I quite distinctly saw Chopper's dad suppress a military salute. She'd certainly got them going. This wasn't a mere sermon. This was a call-to-arms.

And now I understood why Mum had chosen to come a second time to this rousing lecture on Standing By Your Mates and Who Dares Wins. Months of Estelle had knocked the stuffing out of her. Listening to Miss Sullivan thumping her tub was probably the quickest way there was to get herself back on form. I'd never realized before that being a parent was like being in some giant national football team – Parents v. Children – with games scheduled every day. If the parents slack off, then their goal average crashes. Before they know it, they'll be on their way down and out of the league, losing their major fixtures (like drugs and unprotected sex and staying out all night).

Fat chance of that! Wallace School Intermediates' parents looked ready for the comeback, leaping to their feet and stuffing their arms into their coat sleeves. The meeting was over, and they were all raring to go. There was none of the usual hanging about and chatting. They were emptying the hall as smartly as if Miss Sullivan's last ringing cry of 'Goodnight!' was a fire bell.

I nudged Chopper. Sighing, he stubbed out his cigar in an imaginary ashtray, and together we slipped down the balcony staircase and round the long way, past the science rooms, till we reached the back door. Outside, we threaded our way between the dustbins. At the corner by the kitchens I stopped warily in the shadow of the wall.

'Better wait,' I warned Chopper.

He snorted.

'They'll never notice us. Look at them!'

I looked. Chopper was right. I'd never seen anything like it. They were inspired, striding across to their cars with set faces and determined looks. One or two of them even seemed to be practising standing up to themselves in an argument under their breath. 'Twelve o'clock is late. Late, late, *late*! Nobody smokes. *Nobody* drinks. And *nobody* goes to bars and clubs!'

Car doors slammed like machine-gun fire. Engines revved fiercely and tyres screeched. Mum was the first away, shooting off in a cloud of exhaust fumes. I watched the car disappear round the first corner of the narrow lane, and only turned when Chopper tapped my shoulder.

'What's her best time, from here to home?'

I shrugged.

'I don't know. Four minutes? Four and a half?'

He raised his eyebrows.

'I reckon she's going to shave a good bit off that tonight. She's driving like Miss Adulewebe.'

'Bye, Chopper!'

I was off. I didn't fancy trying to explain to Mum exactly where I'd been, and practically my only chance of being in the house before she arrived was if all the traffic lights between school and Beechcroft Avenue miraculously turned red as she approached, and some huge lorry held her up while it backed into the unloading bay at Budgens.

Cars hooted furiously as I weaved down the lane. In fact I nearly got run over several times. The last I saw of Chopper, he was worming his way along the top of the wall, and doing his Randy Cat at me for a goodbye.

Still running like a madman, I yowled back.

Chapter 8

Usually I jump the gate. But you try a four-minute mile from Wallace School to Beechcroft Avenue. Wings on your feet as far as Acacia Lane, maybe; but after that it's uphill all the way. By the time you get to our house you're so exhausted you can barely pick the Muffy-proof lock on the gate and drag yourself through. Forget flying over it. That's for the birds.

Muffy must have been listening for the click. For as I took my first steps across the lawn to peer through the filthy garage window and check I'd really beaten Mum back home, I saw a small bundle of yellow gnome suit hurtling through the back door and over the grass towards me.

I stretched out my arms to scoop her up and swing her around as usual. But, slipping underneath, she threw herself against me.

ANNE FINE

Clasping me round the legs as if I were some giant tree trunk, she clung so tightly that I couldn't move.

I patted her mop of hair.

'Muffy?'

No words, of course. Just an even tighter grip.

'Are Dad and Estelle still arguing?'

She nodded into my upper leg. It's odd the way, though we both grow, we always keep in step. She gets a bit taller. So do I. Some day, of course, I'm bound to stop and she'll keep right on going. But right now it seems that, as far back as I can remember, whenever I've peeled a weeping Muffy away to peer at her more closely, the little slug trails that she's left on me run right across my thigh.

I wiped her nose with a bit of old tissue.

'Is Mum back?'

She shook her head, and gripped me even tighter. Down from Estelle's bedroom window floated the duet we'd heard so many times in the last year.

'Be reasonable, Estelle! You must admit—'

'Stop telling me what to *think*!'

I prised poor Muffy off and held her far enough away to drop on my heels in front of her.

I put out a hand to lift her chin and take a better look. The tear tracks down her face had dried, but she looked pale and tense. I let her back in my arms, and squeezed her hard. She slid her arms in a stranglehold round my neck, and buried her face against me. She smelled of something milky and familiar. For a moment I couldn't think what.

And then I realized. Those two up there had been so wrapped up in their wrangling, neither had even thought to give Muffy any supper. Muffy is four! She's not allowed to light the stove, or open tins, or use a knife alone. So just like me on all those mornings everyone's so busy arguing with Estelle they can't look for lunch money, the poor thing had had to make do with more cornflakes.

And suddenly I was angry.

It came on in a rush, taking me by surprise. Anger's not something I've felt much before, and so, like William Saffery on the day he finally lost his temper, it was a moment or two before I even recognized the growing ball of fury inside me, the tight feeling in my throat. My hands were trembling and my knuckles went white. I was so angry I had to make an effort not to squeeze Muffy so tightly I bruised her.

And I was astonished, too. For anger isn't something I think of as a part of me. High feelings, high voices, high tempers – they're things I usually sit and watch. The Other People Show. I'm certainly not used to them boiling up inside me, rattling me totally, making me wonder at myself and what I might say or do. Don't forget, I'm the steady one, Dad's good lad, Mum's angel, the one on whom they depend. When it comes to flaming tempers, I have almost no experience at all. This is Will Flowers we're talking about here. Yes, Will Flowers. The one you'll usually find sitting quietly in the front stalls, admiring the tantrums of The Famous Estelle.

But ripping through me was a feeling so intense I was amazed at myself. Like Will in his trench, I could have kicked up a storm. Oh, he had better reasons, sure enough. He'd just found out he'd been betrayed in the worst way – by his own country. There he'd been, stumbling round the dug-out one night, chasing a rat, when a stab from his bayonet caught on the corner of a buried bag.

He'd ripped open the mouldering burlap.

'What's in here? *Letters?*'

In the dim light, he peered a little closer.

'My God! They're ours! Letters from *weeks* ago! They never even left the bloody trench!'

Hardly a man looked up. Streaky kept drying his socks over a candle. MacFie's thumbnail closed imperturbably on the louse he'd just taken such care to chase up the seam of his shirt with heat from his own lighted stub. None of the men on the wire-netting bunks bothered to open their eyes. And all the rest, sprawled against heaps of equipment on the floor, carried on snapping their cards down on the biscuit tins they were using for tables, or dragging at their cigarettes and staring silently into space, as if they'd heard nothing more than the persistent drip, drip, dripping around them, or the thudding of shells through the tons of earth above.

Didn't they understand? Or had they already guessed that this was just another of the tricks to keep them quiet before each attack? Give every man the chance to write a letter. He'd seen enough to know this could be his last letter ever. It would take thought. And thought was better spent on sweetheart and family and home than dwelling on what's to be done, and what might happen in the dead of night, when orders run down the line.

'The letters never even left the bloody trench!'

Somebody near him shrugged. For heaven's sake! Either a man comes back – in which case he writes another – or he does not, and his family get a telegram with such grim news they'll hardly care about a letter rotting in a bag somewhere in France. So why is Will beating the slimy walls of the dug-out with his fists, screaming and yelling:

'Just shoved down here, out of sight! Not even sent back behind the line, where they'd be safe! How many more bags are there? How many more?'

He was tearing at the walls with his hands now. The sodden clods of earth showered on everyone.

'Knock it off, Will!'

'Settle down!'

'Bad enough to be trapped in this stinking hole, without some fool fetching the walls down!'

'Bet all the stay-at-homes are dry enough . . .'

The wave of grumbling swept through the dug-out. And all at once it seemed that everyone had his grievance. 'Rats in the bully beef!' 'Dragged through the mud for miles! Couldn't *expect* it to work by the time it reached the unit!' 'Never thought to send fuses with it!' 'Out of wire . . .' But the soothing litany of further complaints did nothing to drain William Saffery's anger. His shoulders heaved. His eyes burned as fiercely as the cigarette from which Asprey was pulling the last drag. And it was with real fury that he spat out the words:

'They think of everything in this bloody war, except how to bloody well end it!'

And I felt just as angry. Angrier. All that was happening in our house might not be so earth-shattering as real war, but we were all miserable enough. My sister was making our home a shambles too! For months and months now we'd been putting up with her bad temper and her arguments, and the fact that she drains every-body's crystals so dry that Muffy and I get scarcely a look in, let alone a fair deal. When was the last time anyone found five minutes to give me some lunch money?

Back in March!

Well, I had suddenly had enough. Call this Estelle growing up? It was more like exploding. I might be a bit of a pain every now and again, growing out of my trousers. She was growing out of herself. 'Too big for her boots,' as Gran says.

And why *should* Muffy and I have to put up with absolutely everything in our house, morning till night, depending on the whims of Estelle? It was ridiculous. There was only one of her, but there were four of us. And look how we ended up spending our time! Mum trying to stiffen her resolve at a meeting, Dad upstairs battling for hours, me peering through peep-holes, and Muffy up well beyond her bedtime, ignored and unfed. I could tell just from looking at her face that she'd been lurking in that doorway, as desperate to hear the click of the garden gate as William Saffery always was to hear the grinding rumble from behind that promised reinforcements.

Well, it's quite flattering to think that, to someone else, you are the cavalry.

Time to live up to the job. I hoisted Muffy in my arms to carry her into the house and plonk her down safely in front of *Rumpelstiltskin*. I was going to tell Dad and Estelle what I thought of them.

But just then, screeching to a halt on wheels behind came more fighting power than I could muster in a thousand years.

Mum.

The ferocious slamming of the car door told

half the tale. And you only had to see the dark look on her face to know that every traffic light between here and Wallace School had turned red as she approached it, and the great Belgian lorry that delivers yoghurts to Budgens had got its back section jammed in the loading bay again, blocking the road at the corner.

Muffy didn't mess around. She stuck her head straight up my jumper. And Mum didn't bother with any amiable warm-up chat. She got straight to the point.

'Where's your sister?'

I nodded upwards to the open window. Phrases from the duet still floated down.

'I can't have a child of mine roaming the streets at that time of night . . .'

'You're not even listening, Dad!'

I turned to Mum. The anger hadn't gone. It had got deeper, redder, wider.

'This has to stop!' I yelled. 'We can't go on like this!'

She turned and stared.

I was amazed at myself, but I kept yelling, really yelling.

'It's like a war! It just goes on and on. It never stops! One long battle going on, day after day, week after week, month after month! How long is it carrying on? Two years? *Three? Four?*'

If I was yelling before, then I was truly bellowing now. Even the voices from the bedroom had fallen silent. I didn't lower my voice. Oh, no. I wanted my father and Estelle to hear. And in my fury, things I didn't even know I thought came tumbling out.

'We need some calm and order in this house!' I was nodding at the bulge in my clothing that was Muffy. 'We need a place to live where people don't have to keep diving up other people's jumpers just to feel a tiny bit safer – not even *safe*. I'll tell you what we need. We all need *peace*.'

Under my jumper, I felt Muffy wriggling.

'Sssh, Will. Ssshh! Doesn't matter.'

But it did. Oh, I've felt a loyalty to Estelle all my life. She's my *sister*. But right now I wanted to see her pushed well and truly back in line. I wanted to see her trounced. Like William Saffery, I'd had enough. And I wasn't prepared to be fobbed off any longer.

'We can't go on like this,' I yelled again. 'I'm sick of it, and Muffy's sick of it.'

I shook her head out of my woolly.

'*Aren't* you?' I demanded, exactly the same way Estelle does.

For a moment I wasn't sure of her support. But then dumbly she nodded, and her eyes filled with tears.

'See?' I crowed. '*See?*'

Silence. Mum didn't speak. There was no sound at all. After a moment or two I heard a little cough from over in next-door's garden. It seemed to break the spell. Mum took a breath and pushed her hair back from her face. She looked at Muffy, then she looked at me. Then, still without saying a word, she turned and walked quickly towards the house.

I shifted Muffy in my arms.

'Come on,' I said grimly. 'We'll watch from the back lines. That is the War Reporter's job, after all. Count them out – count them back.'

I carried her through the kitchen after Mum. We caught up on the stairs. Mum hadn't stopped to knock on Estelle's door. She'd simply stuck out her fist and burst the door open. Muffy and I were just in time to see the look of pure astonishment spread over Dad's face as Mum materialized in the doorway.

Mum spoke first.

'What's going on?'

Her voice was icy calm. Dad wilted visibly beneath her gaze. Estelle scrambled to her feet and glowered horribly.

Mum turned on her.

'Are you still wasting your father's time, going on about this party?'

Dad looked quite horrified. He likes to think that any problem in our family can at least be discussed. Before Estelle could even open her mouth, he'd broken in to defend her.

'Bridget, please! Estelle and I are simply sitting here having a little chat—'

Mum wasn't listening. She steamrollered over him. She mowed him down.

'Because you're not going to go to this party, Estelle. Do you understand? It's as simple as that, and there's no need for any discussion. The whole idea was insane in the first place, and no one in this entire family is going to waste a moment more indulging you by arguing about it. So you can just take off that—'

She pointed to the slinky black blouse that was slipping off Estelle's shoulder. Words failed her.

'That *thing*.'

She lowered her finger to the shredded skirt.

'And *that* thing.'

Down to the fishnet tights.

'And *those*! And you can just stuff them straight into Muffy's dressing-up box, where they belong. And you can get into your nice warm dressing gown and slippers and come downstairs and have your supper before bedtime!'

Dad may have been pretty well speechless. But not Estelle. In her outrage she leaped on the bed. Her black suede boots were on the coverlet. She danced up and down in her rage.

'You can't do this to me! You can't! I'm not a baby any more. You've got to stop treating me like a child!'

She turned to Dad for help.

'Dad! Stop her! You've got to stop her! Nobody else's mother treats them like this. Nobody's! No one else gets stopped all the time. Other people's parents don't go on and on about how late twelve o'clock is, or things like smoking and drinking. Everyone else will be allowed to go to the club!'

I thought I'd been yelling earlier. But, believe me, till you've heard Estelle yell, you've only heard whispering. Estelle's voice can fetch down plaster. She can split walls. Chopper and I aren't joking when we cross our fingers against her for our protection. I tell you, Estelle in a temper is a fiendish sight.

But, just this once, she was outclassed by Mum. I've never seen anything like it. It was astonishing. I had a sudden vision of what Estelle will look like in twenty years. The two seemed so alike. I don't think I've ever really realized before that they share the same black hair, the same green eyes, the same witchy pointing finger.

But Mum's still taller. And Mum's got power. Raising herself to her full height, she turned on Estelle a look so withering I practically shrivelled on the spot, just from the fall-out. She looked for all the world like the Bad Queen in *Snow White* the day the mirror gives her the bad news. The scowl on her face could have cracked glass, the light in her eyes start a forest fire, the steel in her voice cut you down.

The witchy finger pointed deep into Estelle's heart.

'*Nobody* smokes,' declared Mum. '*Nobody* drinks. And *nobody* goes to clubs like *Fiends*!'

Dad's mouth opened – and then promptly shut again. He knows the terms of surrender when they're announced.

So does Estelle. She bounced back down on the

bed, muttering and grumbling like some bad fairy who'd been beaten in a skirmish of spells. Mum left her to it, spinning on her heel and sailing out of the door. As she passed me, she said:

'And as for you . . .'

Even before Muffy clapped her hands over my ears so I couldn't hear it, a dozen possible endings to her sentence were echoing in my brain:

'And as for you, Will Flowers. Think yourself lucky you have a family at all. Why, there are children all over the world who . . .'

'And as for you, don't be such a wimp. Good thing you're not in a real war . . .'

'And as for you, if you had a bit more spirit yourself, you might understand what your sister's going through . . .'

'And as for you . . .'

I clutched the banisters, my head spinning. Was it guilt? It was my fault that Mum had squashed Estelle. Or was it that awful anger back again?

My hands were sweating and I was breathing hard. Even my knees were trembling. I sank down on the top stair, and Muffy slid from my grasp and moved a few steps along the landing, watching me in some alarm.

What on earth was the matter?

And then I realized. Suddenly it all became clear. I realized why, for months, I've been obsessed with William Saffery's book, reading it over and over every night, reading nothing else. I realized why I've let my sister treat this household like a battlefield, and barely said a word when I've fetched up with no help with my homework and stale carrot sandwiches for lunch day after day.

I realized why, until today, I'd never once stood up for what I want: peace, order, and a quiet life.

I am like William Saffery.

I'm a coward.

There. Now it's said. I've got it out at last. What is so brave about going along with things you don't even believe in? It takes no courage to day-dream about what you'll tell the Big Brass when you show them round the battlefield. You know it's not going to happen. Anyone can *dream*. And there's no guts in going over the top, just like a sheep, because other people are watching. Some of them might be people like Estelle, despising you for your weakness. I am beginning to agree with her. If you don't think that what you're doing is not only right, but also sensible, you shouldn't be doing it at all.

That is true valour.

The longer I sat there thinking about William Saffery, the less impressed I was. Having those doubts didn't take much daring, did it? He claimed to be the very eyes and ears of war. He wrote it down, Impeccable War Reporter. He wasn't daft. He saw the whole of it for what it was – a stupid, wasteful mess.

And he did *nothing*. The lines I've read a thousand times swam back in mind. 'I looked around at all these men who had no choice but to stay, and I knew that in my own gift lay my deliverance. All that I had to do was walk back a hundred yards behind the lines, and tell them my real age.'

Why didn't he? It was the longest summer. A hundred thousand times he must have thought about what would happen if he were simply to drop his gun in the mud, walk back from his position on the line, and, taking care that there were plenty of witnesses standing around him, come out with the magic words: 'I'm not eighteen.'

And he didn't even do that. He nursed his comforting secret like one of Muffy's furry bedtime toys, but he hung in there week after murderous week, until the day that blessed shell exploded in front of him, taking his leg off and saving his precious life. But how many other young boys for whom he felt 'no enmity' did he kill in those months? He doesn't say. The last William Saffery saw of France was the same long and winding road that brought him in, unfolding back again, like a grey ribbon. He had got out alive. How many didn't?

I think that I was on the verge of tears. Certainly Muffy was creeping closer and closer, and getting ready to pat me. But suddenly Mum's voice came up the stairs, shattering the silence.

'Will! I thought I told you to put Muffy to bed!'

So *that* was what Muffy hadn't wanted me to hear. 'And as for you . . .' I stared at her reproachfully. She slid her thumb out of her mouth and grinned, before hopping off to her bedroom.

Sighing, I took off after her. At least in our house there's no time to brood. Mum keeps you busy.

And so does Muffy. First time around, I couldn't find her at all. Then I heard scrabbling, and realized she was in one of her cupboards, rooting through stuff on the floor.

'No time to tidy up now. Hop into bed.'

I switched on her frog lamp and opened *Rumpelstiltskin* for the eight billionth time. It's falling apart.

Then she popped up in front of me, a little yellow gnome. Under my nose, she thrust another book.

'What's this?'

She didn't speak, of course. I took a look.

'*Beauty and the Beast*.'

A smile spread over her face.

'Moving on, are we?'

Nodding happily, she slid between the sheets. I bet she thought I'd just fall in with her plans, settling myself against the pillows and starting straight up with the story:

'*Once upon a time, in a faraway kingdom, there lived a rich merchant who had three beautiful daughters . . .*'

Well, no such luck. Muffy might not have realized it yet, but this was the day on which Will Flowers had decided to learn to stand up and be counted.

I closed the book.

'It looks very good. But I'm not reading it until you ask me properly.'

Muffy stared. Then she pointed at the book again.

I ignored her. Whistling softly, I gazed up at the ceiling and pretended to examine the dust on her light fitting.

She stabbed the book again.

The witchy finger holds no terrors for me. Is someone who's been pointed at by Mum with her scarlet fingernails, and Estelle with her green ones, likely to crack when they see a chubby pink finger?

No, I'm afraid they are not.

'I'm sorry,' I told her firmly. 'I'm sick of this business of you not talking to me. I'm not a reading and a carrying machine. I am your brother. Will Flowers is my name. And if you want me to read you a bedtime story, you can go to the trouble of asking me.'

She glowered at me like a tiny Estelle. I'm surrounded by them, all ages and sizes. But I am going to hold firm.

'Go on,' I prompted. 'Make with the words. *Ask* me.'

'Read me a story, please,' she muttered, still glowering horribly.

'Certainly,' I said, bowing and scraping. 'With

the greatest of pleasure. I'd love to read to you. Nothing would be nicer. Would you like this one?' I opened the book to the first page. 'It's called *Beauty and the Beast*.'

She nodded.

I made as if to close the book again.

'Yes, please. That one,' she said.

'Very well,' I said. 'Are you sitting quite comfortably? Then I'll begin. "*Once upon a time, in a faraway kingdom . . .*"'

She snuggled against my shoulder. And I read on. I read aloud to Muffy so often now that I can do it almost without thinking. I do a different voice for every character. I sound scary in all the right places. But often, even as the words come pouring out, my mind is off and away, thinking about the day I've just had, or the one that I'm going to have tomorrow.

And as I read on about the rich merchant stealing the rose from Beast's garden, and being given the chance to go back one last time to say farewell to his family, I couldn't help thinking about Mum and Dad. Neither of them is chicken. And yet they both keep on going day after day, battle by battle, grind by grind. Why haven't they stood up to my dear sister? Is it because they know she's busy doing something useful, fighting all these good fights? Perhaps the last thing they really wanted was to bring up a good lad and a good angel. Maybe they'd like to think they've brought up people who can speak their minds, and make their own decisions. Maybe they know that those with the courage to fling their rifles down and walk away are really very precious. Estelle's always been brilliant at looking after people – everyone's agreed on that. But maybe, these days, she's thinking in bigger terms than just one child like Muffy in her lap, listening to *Rumpelstiltskin*. After all, without people like Estelle, people like me get herded into wars time and again, as if we didn't even realize the value of our own lives.

At least Estelle knows the value of hers. What did she yell at Dad?

'I only get one life!'

Estelle's not daft. William Scott Saffery didn't realize what his life was worth until he fetched up in those holes of hell. Only out there, he said, where death was everywhere, did he come to understand for the first time what he was so close to losing. Sometimes a fierce shaft of energy and hope ran through him, and he felt nothing but alive.

Like a fish in the water, he says. Like a bird in the air.

William Saffery stopped thinking, 'This might not last', and simply lived. And he knew, however short a time his luck might hold, that living was worthwhile. There was a day or two behind the lines when he lay in the shadow of a tree, and watched the bright puffy clouds go floating overhead. He ran his fingertips over the bloom of an apple, and slid his body in the water of the stream, and felt the sun on his back. All simple things he could have done at home, in times of peace. But all made so much more precious because his good friend Chalky had not come back from the last raid, and William knew he himself might not come back from the next one.

William Scott Saffery had to go to war before he even learned—

'Go on!'

'What?'

'You've stopped. You've just stopped reading.'

I stared down at the page. Beauty was leaning over the body of Beast, wringing her hands in despair. Had we got that far already? I carried on.

175

But I had noticed that, to get me reading again, Muffy hadn't prodded me, or stabbed the page. She'd opened her mouth and spoken. Things really were changing.

And maybe that's how Mum and Dad keep on going. Because Estelle's changing, too. Mum can't just be keeping her head down day after day in dumb and senseless endurance. She's not the type. She must have some idea of where Estelle is going, who she'll be, the sort of strong and valuable person who's waiting for us at the end.

'Go on, Will! Read!'

I gave myself a little shake.

'"*And love was rewarded, as love always is. For suddenly the Beast rose to his feet, and was a beast no longer. He had become a glorious prince, whose beauty shone as brightly as the day."*'

Well, maybe that's it! What all Estelle's fans are waiting for! Really, these old fairy stories do hit the spot.

Muffy uncorked her thumb again.

'Will! Don't keep on stopping. Read to the end.'

I read on, through the magnificent wedding, until I reached the bottom of the last page.

'"*And they all lived in happiness and peace."*'

Happiness and peace. Muffy snuggled down,

and I switched off the frog lamp. The old fairy-tale ending. It's the best.

On my way down, I was still thinking about it. And about me. Was I a hopeless case? I'd spoken up once to Mum. And once to Muffy. That might not be quite up to Estelle's shattering goal average, but it was one up on William Saffery. That was a start. Coming down the stairs, I must have picked a leaf or two off the geranium without thinking, because when I heard my name called from the kitchen, I couldn't answer at once. I had a mouthful of greenery.

Then I overheard Dad.

'Will's taking his time, as usual. His supper's curling at the edges. We should have sent Estelle. She reads much faster.'

I caught Mum's voice above the rush of water from the taps.

'But Muffy *adores* Will.'

I stopped dead on the stair. I've gone so long assuming Muffy adores Estelle, and I am second best. I was amazed to learn that in among all the other changes there was a windfall like this. I suppose, thinking back, I must have been a bit dense not to have put two and two together, what with Muffy spending all that time in my lap, and sticking her head up my jumper. But still, I was dead chuffed. I strolled in the kitchen feeling ten feet tall.

And maybe that's the reason I caught my head on the spice shelf, fetching it down with the most tremendous clatter, and setting little tubs and jars rolling all over the floor.

Dad sighed with exasperation when he saw the mess.

'Bridget, I thought you put that shelf a good three inches higher up the wall last time he knocked it down.'

'It's not my fault,' Mum said irritably. 'The boy must still be growing.'

'For heaven's sake!'

Both of them glowered at me. I glowered back. I was about to say, 'Excuse me for living!' when I was interrupted.

'Don't pick on Will! People can't help it if they grow! If it's anyone's fault he's getting so tall, it's yours. Who made him eat all those sensible meals, and drink his milk, and take his vitamins? You did! So don't start trying to make him feel crummy just because he's growing like hogweed!'

Estelle to the rescue. Very nice for me. I turned on her to complain.

'I am not growing like hogweed! I'm simply reaching my full height.'

But at her first sight of my face, she'd burst out laughing. I peered in the mirror by the sink. Last time this happened, I was turmeric yellow. The time before, I was paprika pink. This time I was speckled all over with greeny-grey flakes of dried thyme. I looked about a hundred years old.

But, then again, Estelle didn't even look like a human being. She was wearing her dressing gown and slippers, but so far she'd only wiped the make-up off one eye. She looked like a pirate raccoon in a fluffy pink coat with matching booties.

I burst out laughing back.

Furious, she reached down for the nearest little spice tub, and hurled it. It caught me neatly just above the ear. The top flew off, and I was covered with cinnamon. Little rivulets of the stuff cascaded down my neck.

I was livid. To pay her back, I threw the bag of garam masala. It split the moment it hit her. She went a browny-grey colour on the spot.

'Estelle! Will! Stop it at once!'

To be fair, it wasn't Estelle's fault that Dad caught her arm, spoiling her aim, just as she hurled the baking powder. Off came the lid, and a cloud of white floated down gently on Mum.

Mum's got no patience at all. She quite deliberately snatched up the chilli pepper and threw it at Dad.

That really annoyed him, you could tell. He threw the rosemary. Mum fought back with bicarbonate of soda. He hurled powdered ginger. She pelted him with cloves and peppercorns. He tipped dried mustard over her head.

Estelle and I stared as the floor tiles vanished under sheets of greeny-grey with colourful speckled patches. The walls had gone a sort of mixed spice colour. The mess was terrible. You could tell, just from looking, that it was going to take a week to clear things up. But just as Mum and Dad stopped flinging things at one another, and came to their senses, there was an interruption. A proud voice in the doorway said:

'Everyone look at me!'

We all turned. You'd think if anything would make Dad laugh, it would be Mum with her new ginger hair, or pink-coated one-eyed Estelle, or even me – Old Father Thyme.

But, no. What set him off was the sight of

Muffy dressed in Estelle's party gear. The slinky blouse slid so far off her shoulders it looked like a ratty black vest. The shredded skirt hung almost to her feet. The tights fell in giant wrinkles around her ankles. Muffy looked like an orphan who had been rooting in people's dustbins to find something to wear.

Mum and Dad clutched one another. I kept my face straight, but it was difficult.

It was Estelle, of course, who piped up first.

'Muffy, those are my clothes!'

Muffy pouted, but she didn't speak.

I wasn't having that. I'd won this battle. We weren't going back. I gave Muffy a very clear warning look. 'Make with the words,' it said.

She took a breath, and spoke up forcefully.

'Mum said you had to give them to me. For my dressing-up box.'

Silence. The sheer astonishment of hearing Muffy speaking up like that had even shaken Estelle. I saw Mum glance at Dad. They looked delighted. Then Mum stepped in as fast as possible to stop the New Talking Muffy getting mashed in an argument with Estelle. Though you could almost see the words choking Mum as she came out with them, it was clearly Peace At Any Price time at 27 Beechcroft Avenue.

'Oh, Muffy! It was so silly of me to say that. You see, Estelle's clothes belong to her, and she's such a grown-up girl now that what she wears is really her own business. I can't force her to put her clothes in your dressing-up box.'

You should have seen Estelle's face. Talk about Victory! But Muffy's crumpled till I thought she was about to cry.

Dad leaped in, waving his own olive branch.

'Muffy, I'll tell you what. I'll give Will two pounds, and on the way back from taking you to the puppet show tomorrow, he'll chum you into the charity shop and you can choose whatever you like off the fancy rail for your dressing-up box.'

I stared. I hadn't realized that my plans for Saturday had been so carefully worked out. Puppet show. Babysitting. Jumble hunt. The old Will might simply have thought quietly and sarcastically to himself that it was a good thing one of them happened to mention it all in his hearing, otherwise he might have made the serious mistake of assuming his Saturday was his own. The new Will had other plans.

The words were only halfway to the front of my mouth when Estelle pounced.

'Dad! You can't just—'

I can pounce, too. I clapped my hand over my sister's mouth.

'You can't just plan my weekend for me,' I told Dad, all by myself. 'You have to *ask*.'

Everyone stared at me. They were amazed. I nearly cracked, but then Dad looked at Mum, who shrugged, and asked me courteously:

'Will, would you mind?'

Easy, when you know how! I felt so proud.

'Fine by me,' I declared.

Muffy spoke up again.

'Oh, goody. I do love puppets.'

Mum looked thrilled. Dad slid his arm round her shoulders. Bicarbonate of soda flew up in the air, and he shed peppercorns and cloves. Estelle patted the front of her dressing gown, puffing out garam masala. I shook my head, and a shower of dried thyme fell around me.

Hastily, Dad took charge.

'Nobody move!'

He turned to Muffy, who was still standing safely in the doorway.

'You're the only one who can save us, Muffy.

Follow my orders exactly. Go up and fetch four towels . . .'

She turned to go. Then she turned back and asked him cheekily,

'Can I have ice cream at the puppet show?'

Dad splattered spice in all directions as he moved threateningly towards her.

And Muffy fled.

Chapter 9

The weekend was murder. Wall-washing. Floor-mopping. Lightbulb-wiping. I thought I'd be glad to get away, but school on Monday turned out even worse. Someone must have washed my school shirt in some fierce new detergent to get rid of the cinnamon and thyme. (Believe it or not, my skin's very sensitive.) I'd hardly stood through the first two or three notices in Assembly before the itching began.

I scratched and scratched. I scratched through French and maths, and through geography (till Mr Astley threw me out). I spent the rest of that period in the cloakrooms with my shirt off, but wasted what should have been half an hour's glorious relief by having a really good scratch.

By the time I joined Chopper in the dining hall at lunchtime, the top half of my body was seriously aflame.

He watched me pouncing on the worst places for a bit, then offered his advice.

'You shouldn't scratch. It only makes it worse.'

Rather than hit him, hard, I told him all about the Spice War at home. He listened, rapt, then he said thoughtfully:

'I reckon your family's cracking up.'

'Cracking up?'

'Yes,' he said. 'Buckling under the strain.'

Reaching across, he lifted my untouched sandwich out of my lunchbox and peeled the two halves apart.

'For example,' he said, 'there's nothing in this sandwich. Only salad cream.'

'That's because it's a salad cream sandwich.' (Beggars can't be choosers.)

Sadly he shook his head.

'There's no such thing. And it shouldn't be in your lunchbox. Someone your size needs proper food.'

I wasn't going to argue with that, was I? That was my opinion too. And I'd been saying it all term. But I wasn't sure that I wanted to hear it from Chopper.

'Things in your own house can't be so brilliant. You have to argue with your parents for a week to stay out long enough to see a film.'

Chopper looked smug.

'No, I don't. That's all finished.'

Pigs can fly . . .

'Oh, yes?'

'Yes.'

He took to waving his fresh crusty thick Italian roll in front of my face as he went on to explain. Great juicy slices of salami kept dropping out of it. I picked them up and popped them into my mouth. They were delicious. It was so long since I'd had anything worth eating at the paupers' table that I let Chopper ramble on for quite a while before I realized he was saying something that could prove mighty useful in our house.

'What was all that again?'

He went over it once more.

'When Dad's away, Mum and I settle between us what time I have to be back. Eleven o'clock, say. She sets the alarm clock for five past eleven and puts it outside her room. I creep in dead on eleven and switch the alarm off before it wakes her. Then I reset it for her crack of dawn start. Hey, presto! I get to see the end of the film, and Mum doesn't have to lie there worrying in case she falls asleep before it's time to wake up and worry about me.'

I had a bit of a scratch while I took all this on board.

'What happens if you get home late and the alarm goes off?'

Chopper's face darkened.

'She says that since she's sure I would never dream of breaking an agreement, naturally she'd phone the police at once.' The scowl deepened. 'And she would, too . . .'

I shook my head in wonder.

'Brilliant. Absolutely brilliant.' A nasty thought struck. 'Did you think it up yourself?'

He looked embarrassed.

'Found it in a book.'

This was a newsflash indeed: Chopper Reads!

'What book?'

He blushed.

'*Coping with the Awkward Adolescent.* My mother picked it up at some branch library sale.'

Oh, ho. The District Barbarian flinging away more gems. She clearly hadn't changed. But it did seem to me as if everyone else who lives within five square miles of Wallace School had suddenly decided to get a grip. How many things had changed almost overnight? I'd stood up to everybody in my family. Muffy was making with the words. And now here was my mate Chopper (who hasn't voluntarily opened a book since he had gloves on elastic in his sleeves) suddenly culling bright ideas from his recreational reading, and slotting them usefully into family life. He'd even managed to upgrade his manky lunches till they were practically haute cuisine. So why should I skid to a halt after Battle No. 1? They say that every victory brings another. Roll on the next big fight. It was time to solve all my other problems. For instance, I could insist on taking a few notes off Dad each time he goes to the bank. I could take responsibility for getting them changed myself. Then I'd have lunch money every day – no fuss, no bother. Or I could even add things to the weekly shopping list so, if I had to pack one, there would be something to pack.

It was a novel thought. I had a bit of a scratch as I worked out the details. And it occurred to me as well that if I was no longer having to trail round the house every morning before school, begging for lunch money, the rest of my family probably wouldn't get on my nerves quite so much as they do now, and I might not get on theirs.

The pleasant notion of early-morning sunshine at 27 Beechcroft Avenue, inside and out, was interrupted by Chopper. He'd stuffed the last of his crusty roll into his mouth, and embarked on a precis of his recent reading.

'In this book about the awkward adolescent,' he told me indistinctly, chewing hard, 'it says the childhood personality has to break down, so that a new one can grow.'

Weird.

'What? Like shaking a kaleidoscope to get a new pattern?'

'I suppose so. Or shuffling a pack of cards for a fresh game.'

'I see.'

I stared across the room. Estelle was using both hands to plait Marisa's hair, while Flora posted chips in her mouth for her. I had a bit of a think as I scratched, hard. It certainly did seem a pretty good description of what had been happening to my sister. Was I the next in line? Late bloomer, as usual. Still one year older, and still one behind.

She moves in first, the strong attacking force. I follow after, the steady mopping-up operation. How many battles would I have to fight? And how would I end up?

Chopper was chuntering on.

'Mind you, in your house sometimes it sounds as if everyone's personality is breaking down.'

Scratch! Scratch! It was hard to think. But on the whole I reckoned Chopper was on the wrong track with this one. Things at home weren't that bad. No one was cracking up. Mum and Dad go off their rockers from time to time. But generally they press on very well. They still shop. We still eat. They pay the bills. You can't say fairer than that. William Scott Saffery saw men so badly shattered that nothing and no one would ever put them to rights again. They had collapsed on the field. They had become as deaf to the taunts and threats of their officers as they were to the sympathy of their mates. They were even in-different to the fear of court martial (which as everyone knew meant little more than a swift bullet in the head). They had lost hope. The living world had proved so terrible that they no longer cared which side of the mad equation was wiped away: the horrors around them – or them.

No, things were nowhere near that bad. Maybe Mum sometimes hides in the garage, or climbs through the window, or Muffy sticks her head up a jumper. So what? If someone in a family has worked out that it's time to change a bit into the person that they want to be, then one or two other people in that family might end up with battle fatigue. What's wrong with that? Some battles are worth fighting. I've learned that from Estelle.

Estelle . . .

I took a peep at her while I was scratching. Flora caught my eye, and stuck her tongue out automatically. Then she bent down and whispered in Estelle's ear. Estelle's busy hands kept on plaiting, but she glanced in my direction. Then she looked again, and said something to Flora.

Flora said something back.

Estelle flipped the elastic band onto Marisa's plait, doubling it till it was tight. Then, popping the last chip into her mouth, she strolled across to me.

'Flora says you must have lice.'

I stopped scratching at once.

'Nonsense.'

Estelle's like Mum. She never stops to discuss

things. Quick as a flash, she reached down and pushed my unbuttoned sleeves high up my wrists.

The rash was fierce.

'That is awful, Will.'

'It's all right,' I said. 'It isn't bothering me.'

(I must be mad. I was in *misery.*)

Shrugging, Estelle turned and went back to her table. I looked at Chopper, who was staring at me as if I were unhinged. Suddenly it was as if all the things I'd learned about myself at the weekend swept back over me in force. This business of changing inside is not quite as simple and straightforward as growing out of your trousers, I can tell you. You can't depend on it. It comes in waves.

Late bloomer I may be; hopeless I'm not.

I stood up and started unbuttoning my shirt.

Chopper was still staring.

'Go on,' I ordered him. 'Take it off.'

'What?'

'Your shirt. Take it off. My skin's very sensitive, and yours isn't. I want to swap shirts.'

He started to argue, but I cut him off.

'Look, Chopper,' I said. 'I can't stand sitting here suffering quietly any longer. So take your shirt off, please.'

193

Chalky made William Saffery swap boots with him once, for very similar reasons. I thought that was dreadful when I read it first. Now I think I understand.

Chopper could tell I meant it. He stood up. Together we unbuttoned. You don't realize how many people are watching you in a public place, till you do something unusual. I was hardly down to my navel before the shouting and the stamping began. The noise in the lunch hall is always tremendous. This took it over the top. I was a bit embarrassed. After all, I didn't look too fetching, inflamed in great blotchy patches. But Chopper was clearly enjoying the attention, the same way he got a buzz out of it that time we set all the parents off in the school hall.

'Thank you,' he said, bowing to left and right, and flexing his puny muscles. 'Thank you so much. Thank you.'

Amongst all the cries of 'More! More!' and 'Get 'em off!' there were complaints that people at the hatch end couldn't see. Chopper cooperatively climbed on a chair.

'Thank you. You are so kind. Thank you, one and all.'

Miss Sullivan's voice cut through his like a wire through cheese.

'Rupert Murgatroyd Chopperly! Get off that chair at once!'

It isn't fair, using someone's real name as if it's a lethal weapon. A ripple of sympathy ran through the hall. Chopper went pale, and climbed down from the chair. He wouldn't look at her, and she knew better than to push her luck. She just strode out of the hall, and the faint hissing that had greeted her spite grew into a crescendo as she disappeared again through the swing doors.

When I looked back, Flora, Marisa and Estelle were standing in front of us.

'That was *brilliant*, Chopper,' said Flora.

'Your muscles are *huge*,' said Marisa.

'You showed the Old Bag,' said Estelle.

Girls are so *nice*. The colour flooded back to Chopper's face.

'Ta, Flora. Ta, Marisa. Ta, Stelly – I mean, Estelle.'

She favoured him with the amazing smile that hasn't been sighted in our house for weeks.

'That's all right, Chopper. You can call me Stelly, since you're so used to it.'

I still wouldn't chance it myself, not on one

of her bad days. But Chopper looked pretty thrilled.

Estelle turned to me.

'Here,' she said. 'Catch!'

I caught it. It was a tin of skin cream. 'Jojoba and cucumber' it said on the lid. 'Soothing and safe.'

'Don't use it all,' she ordered. 'Flora says it's wonderful.'

It was. I'd hardly rubbed a little in the worst places before my skin cooled down. Chopper claimed that the skin cream was useless, and the real cure was swapping shirts with him. I didn't care. The only thing that mattered was the great glorious relief of stopping itching. I felt like a fiery furnace cooling down. In the sheer delirium of my reprieve, I ate the last salad cream sandwich I ever intend to eat in my whole life.

Meanwhile, Chopper was staring blindly after Marisa, Flora and Estelle, who were ambling out of the lunch hall.

'Do you think she meant what she said?' he asked suddenly.

'Who?'

He stared at me.

'Marisa, of course.'

I nearly choked.

'*Marisa?*'

A seraphic smile spread over his face. I honestly think it must have been because I said her name. I was appalled. I may not have bothered to mention it too often, but Chopper isn't *stupid*. Surely he realized that what Marisa said about his muscles was simply a bit of moral support for someone who had the misfortune to be named Rupert Murgatroyd Chopperly. Not that I'm claiming Chopper is a wimp. Anyone who can share a home with the man who runs 'Start Orienteering', and live to tell the tale, has to have inner resources.

But muscles? No.

What's a friend for, if not to put you straight at the right moments?

'Chopper—' I pedalled off. But he wasn't listening.

'And did you see the way Stelly had plaited her hair for her?'

'Chopper!'

'It's not really plain brown at all. It's more a sort of tawny—'

'*Chopper!*'

He pulled himself together, and stood up.

'Anyhow,' he said. 'I'd better get off after them, to thank Marisa for the skin cream.'

'The skin cream belongs to *Flora*.'

But he'd gone.

Chapter 10

Leaving me on my own. Which is exactly how I've stayed over the last three days. I'm not that bothered. Chopper's passions never last for long, and I reckoned I could do with a day or two of peace and quiet before I welly in about this lunch money, and better fillings for my sand-wiches, and all the other things I'm going to be changing around here.

But I've made good use of the time, getting this war report brought up to date. Count them out. Count them back. If Chopper hasn't come to his senses by the end of next week, I might log him down as one of the lost. But right now he's still simply Missing In Action.

And I'm holed up here for the very last time. There's not much else to write. I could keep on, of course. One of the things I've learned is that

Miss Adulewebe was quite right. Once you've got your bum on a seat, it's downhill all the way. You can write about almost anything. But I'd quite like to get back to reading other people's books now. I have a whole pile down beside the bed. I've even found another Alec Whitsun (Alicia Whitley must keep herself busy!) – a nice change from carnage and war.

And there's another good reason. THE BESHOOHOEFTE BANK is pretty well filled up. If I don't stop, I'll end up scribbling round the margins like Gran does on postcards. Better to knock off now. And I don't even have to worry any more about The Curse of Miss Adulewebe falling on my head, because, flicking back, I see that I've even said quite a lot about how I feel.

In fact, I've written a whole book. That's pretty amazing.

And kept it hidden from Estelle. That's more amazing still. I go all hot and cold when I think what would happen if she came across it now. She's been a whole lot more friendly since I had my first stand-up argument with Mum and Dad, but she'd still have my ears off. She'd mash my spleen. Banshee Out of the Basket! I'd be much safer if it were out of the house, but while

Chopper's so pally with Marisa (chum of Flora, chum of The Famous Estelle), it certainly can't go to his house.

What can I do?

Where is the best place for a book if you want to keep it out of everyone's hands?

A publisher! Of course! Alicia Whitley claimed the firm who do all her Alec Whitsuns are slower than snails, and nothing you send them ever comes back for months. That'll be *perfect*. I'll wrap it up, and post it tomorrow afternoon. I won't tell them my real name, in case there's a mix-up, and they go ahead and publish it by mistake. I'll choose a pen name.

And I'll take a leaf out of Alicia Whitley's book. She chose a male name. Very clever, that. I'll choose a female name – a plain one no one will even notice.

I'll pick Anne. And since it's a pretty good book for someone my age – well, I think William Saffery would have liked it – I'll call myself Anne Good. No. Too prissy. Anne Best? Worse. Sounds too boastful. How about Anne Fine?

Yes, Anne Fine. That'll fool Estelle.

And that only leaves the title. No problem there. It won't take long to peel all the gold letters off the front of THE BESHOOHOEFTE BANK, and shift them round until they spell the title I had in mind right from the start.

THE BOOK OF THE BANSHEE

That's it, then. Brilliant!